Hidden Intentions 2

Hidden Intentions 2

Meisha Camm

www.urbanbooks.net

Urban Books, LLC
97 N18th Street
Wyandanch, NY 11798

Hidden Intentions 2 Copyright © 2010
Meisha Camm

ISBN 13: 978-1-60162-414-X
ISBN 10: 1-60162-414-7

First Mass Market Printing June 2014
First Trade Paperback Printing June 2010
Printed in the United States of America

10 9 8 7 6 5 4 3 2 1

Distributed by Kensington Publishing Corp.
Submit Wholesale Orders to:
Kensington Publishing Corp.
C/O Penguin Group (USA) Inc.
Attention: Order Processing
405 Murray Hill Parkway
East Rutherford, NJ 07073-2316
Phone: 1-800-526-0275
Fax: 1-800-227-9604

Dedication

This book is dedicated to all of my fans.

Acknowledgments

I want to thank Jesus Christ for giving me this gift of writing. With the power of prayer and determination, anything is possible.

The easiest part of a book is actually writing it. I have learned struggle, hard work, and patience are three vital elements in the process of becoming successful.

Thank you to Carl Weber, Natalie Weber, and the Urban Books family for believing in my work, once again.

Most importantly, a special thanks goes out to all of the fans. Thank you for the feedback and encouragement.

Thank you to my parents Rodney and Shelly Camm, my daughter, Shamaya, and my sister, Melanie for the encouragement and support. To Jessica Tilles and Niko Hamm—thank you for pushing and pushing me to write to the best of my ability and critiquing my work.

Acknowledgments

To my friends and family—Mr. and Mrs. Ballinger, Tiffany Ballinger, Carla Harrison, Malita Manning, Daneisha Elsbery, Kisha Bailey, Vickie Kennedy, Janie Harrison, Raena and Steven Simmons, Kisha Dodson, Tracy Davis, Carl Davis, Chrissy Smith, Sara Schiable, Linda Potts, Pat Howell, Kisha Powell, Vera Redd, the entire Wade family, Darrick Person, and Renee Bobbs—thank you for your kinds words of encouragement.

To the online writing groups—RealSistaWriters and Writersrx—thank you for always sending me important information pertaining to the book world. A special thanks to Gevell Wagner for taking the time out to read my work.

To Nikki Turner, Tobias Fox, Edwin and Earnest Mcnair, Michael Baisden, Shannon Holmes, Zane, and Mary Monroe— thank you for steering me in the right direction.

Chapter 1

Maybe I shouldn't have agreed to work Lola's shift. *Will I make it through the day?* I wondered, pinning my hair into a bun and looking at my reflection in a peach bra and panty set in the slightly fogged bathroom mirror. My eyes were bloodshot.

"Morning, baby," Tory whispered into my ear after getting out the shower, a blue towel wrapped around his waist.

"Hey." I turned around to give him a peck on the lips then turned to face the mirror again.

"What time do you have to be at work?" Tory began kissing the back of my neck and sliding his hands up and down my arms.

I already knew where this was heading. I turned to face him. "Soon. I want to be to work thirty minutes early. We have new interns starting and I want to set a positive example for them," I explained as he took my bra off.

"You know it turns me on to see you getting ready for work." He guided my panties to the floor then started massaging my left breast with his right hand, his left playing with my clitoris.

"Tory," I cooed, "don't make me late."

"Let me give what you really need." He then turned me around and jammed his python into my pussy.

Tory giving it to me from the back was exactly what I needed to get me through the day. He caressed my inner thighs as he gave me long, hard, and steady strokes. Holding on tight to the bathroom marble countertop wasn't easy.

Before long, I came, and so did he. That felt so damn good. My baby hit the spot, leaving me breathless, and my knees weak. I was ready for an after-orgasm nap.

Chapter 2

"Tonight, I have a surprise for you," Tory announced as we headed toward the truck.

Besides the occasional "I-feel-fat" feeling, mixed with bloating, and more than four sixteen-hour shifts a month at the hospital, things were going well for me. My life couldn't get any better. Once a month, Tory and I took an entire weekend to ourselves. We turned the BlackBerrys off and didn't dare log on to our laptops. Being able to spend time alone and get some much-needed rest was a true luxury.

"Where are you taking me?" I asked buckling my seatbelt.

I was wearing my infamous grape-colored velour set with dark grey New Balance sneakers. Tory secretly desired to burn it. I wore it every chance I got. It was my most comfortable outfit. I was into fashion just as much as the next woman, but I wasn't willing to squeeze myself into some tight-ass clothes just to look good. Those sixteen-hour shifts on my feet at the hospital taught me that sacrificing comfort over style and fashion was a no-no.

"Baby, please do what you do best and ride in the passenger seat!" Tory snickered as he pulled out of the driveway.

Tory had upgraded to a silver Range Rover truck with the complete luxury package, GPS and all. I didn't believe in high monthly car payments, but we had budgeted for the vehicle to be paid off in two years and had one more year to go. I couldn't wait to click the enter button and submit the last payment to Online Bill Pay.

As soon as that car's paid off, we can celebrate, I thought. One of those payments could pay for a cruise and a roundtrip airfare to the island of St. Lucia for the both of us. If I know Tory though, he'll try to convince me to buy another car instead of going anywhere.

I still had my Camry, which Tory had been nagging me to get rid of for something else. Another "something else" hadn't been through thick and thin with me. Besides, it was the sentimental value. My parents had bought me that car. Not to mention, Toyotas, especially Camrys, hold their value.

"Whatever. I do my one-third of driving," I replied, a slight grin on my face, folding my arms across my chest.

"We both know that. I'm just playing." Tory kept his left hand on the wheel as his right hand caressed my thigh.

"You're supposed to drive. Daddy did it for Mommy. It's what you're supposed to do."

"Who said?"

"I'm saying it. This is Nya's world, and you're a key player in it."

"Hmm. Is that so?"

"Yeah." I nodded.

"Well, I guess I'm going to have to step up to the plate and honor your driving rules."

We both busted out laughing.

"I love you," I whispered.

"I love you too," he said, popping in a John Coltrane CD.

Chapter 3

"So this is the place you've been keeping a secret?" I felt the crisp autumn air when I hopped out of the truck. I should've have put on a jacket.

"Yup. Until now. I want to show you the place, you know, to see what you think." He grabbed my right hand to lead the way.

Tory was a silent partner in Thai Temple, a new Thai restaurant at the Loehmann's Plaza Shopping Center in Virginia Beach. His college buddy, Rome, had the idea, and Tory had put up fifty percent of the finances. I loved to see my man venturing out in other projects.

Dressed in an orange polo shirt and jeans, Tory was looking quite handsome. I was having one of those moments where I was grateful he was all mine. We had our moments where I wasn't feeling so grateful, but the feeling was only temporary.

"It doesn't look open. When is the grand opening?"

"For us, it's tonight." Tory placed the key in the door. Upon entering, he entered the code for the Brink's security system.

"All right." I snickered.

"Let me give you a tour."

When I first walked in, I noticed a fish mural on the left-hand side. A little farther in was the bar area, complete with any alcohol and champagne a customer could ask for. To the right was the dining area, which held ten booths and ten tables, ranging from small to large.

The smell of his Unforgivable cologne lingered in the air. The kitchen was spacious, clean, and came with the latest appliances. Thai décor, with photos, artwork, lamps, and sculptures, was displayed throughout the entire restaurant. Most of all, I really admired the light fixtures. Eventually we ended up back at the bar.

"Did you hear that noise?" I turned my head back toward the kitchen.

"Yeah. It's your surprise. Follow me." Tory looked at a text on his cell phone.

"What are you up to?"

"Just wait and see," he said as we entered through the kitchen doors.

"Aah," a man called out and extended his hand to me. "This must be Nya."

"Nya, this is Rome, part-owner and one hundred percent chef of the restaurant."

"Nice to meet you," I said, giving him a hand-shake.

"Likewise, Nya. You are very beautiful." Rome put on an apron. "This man doesn't stop talking about you. I feel as if I've known you for some time." Rome wore a black T-shirt with light blue jeans and black Converse. His hair was spiky, and he had a nice set of pearly white teeth.

"Thank you very much. If I may ask, who came up with your name?"

"My father is from Thailand, and my mother is Italian. Her favorite city is Rome."

"Interesting."

Tory butted in. "So are we ready to get started?"

"Get started with what?"

"Well, I'm going to show both of you how to cook. Your husband picked some pretty good choices. On the menu for tonight, we're preparing spring rolls for an appetizer, pad thai with chicken and shrimp for you, Nya. Plus, beef siam with fresh steamed broccoli and white rice for Tory.

"Hmm. I'm getting hungry already," I said, grabbing aprons for Tory and I from the counter. "Let's get started."

Chapter 4

"Rome, thanks for everything," Tory said.

"The food was great. Maybe, I might cook this at home. Plus, it wasn't as hard as I thought it would be," I added after washing the last dish.

"You're right. It's really not. Time, effort, and nothing but fresh ingredients make a meal delicious. Nya, it was a pleasure meeting you."

"Likewise."

"Tory, I'll touch base with you next week. Thirty days till the grand opening!" Rome exclaimed and took a deep breath.

"It's going to fly by. All the kinks have been worked out with the permits. The hardest one was getting the liquor license and that's in the past. Let's look toward the future of this place becoming the hottest spot for Thai cuisine in the Hampton Roads area of Virginia."

"All right, man." Rome smiled, shook hands with Tory, and let himself out the back door.

***

"Thank you, baby," I whispered almost in tears. "This was so nice."

Lately, I'd been getting teary-eyed at the slightest thing. I wasn't this way before. It must have had something to do with the new birth control I was taking.

"You're welcome. It's not often we get to cook together."

"Yeah, it's not often we get to be together," I hinted in his ear, taking off his belt and kissing him on the lips.

After sliding his jeans and boxer shorts down his ankles, I looked up, gave him a devilish grin, and put his python into my mouth. His head rolled back while he gently caressed the back of my head. Switching from deep-throating him to just sucking the top of his dick drove him crazy.

Soon after, Tory lifted me up and sat me on the countertop. He quickly took off my pants and cranberry-colored thong and wasted no time entering my soaking pussy. While giving me deep thrusts, he hoisted up my shirt and matching colored bra to stare at my breasts. He loved seeing my plump melons bounce up and down. Once he grabbed one, I quickly tightened my vagina around his dick, ready to come.

"Nya, damn! Hmm! I'm about to come!"

"I know you want to," I said, looking into his eyes.

We came together. Both of us needed it, to relieve tension, I especially, since working many hours made my body very stiff.

"Thank you for helping me christen the restaurant. Next time, I want it from the back with you bent over a booth," Tory said before collapsing on my chest.

I giggled. "You're welcome anytime."

Chapter 5

An aroma of hot cocoa lingering in the air and the sounds from the television cooking show, *Turn Up the Heat with G. Garvin*, woke me up. I waited for a commercial to come on then hurried to the bathroom to brush my teeth and wash my face. His version of bacon-wrapped scallops, surf and turf, and chocolate mousse was just a few of the recipes I'd tried. I think I was becoming a great cook. At least, Tory seemed to like whatever was on his plate. The real test was my father though, a picky eater who didn't eat just anyone's food. Golden Corral and whatever Mommy decided to feed him suited him just fine.

Tory entered the bedroom with a bunch of goodies in his hands just as I was making up the bed. "Good morning, sweetheart."

"Hey." I gave him a peck on the lips. Hot cocoa with three marshmallows and a touch of vanilla in one of my favorite snowman mugs, grilled ham, grits with a small slather of butter, and a crisp Belgian waffle drizzled with syrup awaited me. "Thank you."

"You're welcome. Since I've been so busy, I don't get the pleasure of making you breakfast in bed. Nya, things are going to change. Since completing my last project, work is going to slow down for me anyway. Irvin is surprised you haven't divorced me yet."

"Well, I've been working long hours too. I miss our time together, but I know it will not always be like this."

"Drug Aid called you and left a voice mail to pick up your birth control. Now, I don't think you'll be needing it."

"Me either. You'll be a daddy in no time, with my fertile behind." I nestled in his arms.

"Eat up, Mrs. Sothers. Before I cooked you breakfast, I went to the gym, but I still want to take a quick run around the neighborhood. I laid out an exercise outfit with a sweatshirt for you, along with your running sneakers. I know how easy it is for you to get cold." Tory pointed to the clothes on the couch.

Yes, I'd married a closet gym junkie. Tory didn't act like this at first, but after a year, I started noticing he was going to the gym every day. It seemed like he couldn't function unless he did. He claimed it was his way of getting out most of his frustrations.

I'd always said I could never be with someone who needed to work out every day, but now I didn't mind, because I was reaping the benefits of having muscles all over my body.

Chapter 6

Tory and I strolled past the ticket counter at the packed MacArthur Center mall. It was the premiere night for the movie *American Gangster*. I was relieved that I'd purchased the tickets online.

Ten years ago, a movie ticket would have cost $5.75. *Those were the days*, I thought, entering theatre number four.

After I'd gulped down half of my cherry Slush Puppie and took a few bites of lightly buttered popcorn, people started entering in droves. I made a mental note of the sneak previews of *The Spiderwick Chronicles*, *Chronicles of Narnia: Prince Caspian*, *The Eye*, and Ice Cube's latest, *First Sunday*, to see once they were released.

"Did you like the movie?" I asked Tory as we were heading to the car.

"Loved it."

"Me too."

"It's almost that time." He looked down at his watch before paying the parking toll.

"I can't wait for an all-night marathon of *CSI: Miami*."

I turned up the volume on the radio to John Legend's song, "Again."

Twenty minutes later, we were home and getting ready for our late-night marathon.

"Did you have a chance to go to the store and pick up a bottle of rainbow sprinkles?" I inquired, rummaging through the pantry.

"Nya, I'm sorry. Completely forgot about it. While you were visiting your parents earlier, I stayed home and took a nap. I meant to go after I woke up, but it slipped my mind. Let me go right now and get you a bottle. I need to pick up some more Edy's chocolate chip cookie dough ice cream anyway. I ate the last scoop on Thursday night."

"It's all right. You don't have to. We'll go tomorrow." I shrugged my shoulders.

"I'll be right back. Farm Fresh is around the corner," Tory said, putting his jacket on.

Almost two hours later, Tory still hadn't come back. I was just about to dial his cell phone for what seemed like the hundredth time when the house phone rang.

"Hello," I answered on the first ring.

"Nya, I'm glad you're up!" Steven, Tory's older brother, exclaimed.

"What's wrong?" I was getting a horrible feeling deep down in my stomach.

"There's been a terrible accident. I'm right outside in your driveway. Come with me so we can go to the hospital."

"What happened to Tory?"

"I'll explain everything I know when you get in the car."

Thankfully, I still had my clothes on. Desperate to know how my future would be impacted, I almost fell, hurrying down the stairs, but somehow managed to get outside of my house in one piece.

Chapter 7

Dark clouds and a mist of heartfelt sorrow filled the air as hundreds of people gathered at Mount Grove Harvest Church. Now, standing at the gravesite alongside Evelyn and Anne, Tory's mother and sister, I was wondering how we made it through the closed-casket service. Not one, but two portraits of him hung in the church. Numbness, and thinking this was a bad dream that I desperately wanted to wake up from best described how I felt.

I couldn't get out of my head the preacher chanting over and over again, "Instead of mourning, let's celebrate his life."

I just wanted to ask God, "Why did he die? And why now?"

It was complete silence in the car while driving to the gravesite.

Looking down as the funeral workers lowered his bronze, gold-trimmed casket into the grave, I couldn't celebrate. His life was cut too short.

He's gone, I thought, wiping my eyes with the eleventh tissue today.

Tory's father, George H. Sothers, had died of a massive heart attack, which happened while he was sitting in his favorite La-Z-Boy recliner. He'd tried to get up and dial 9-1-1, but Evelyn found him face down in the living room. He was later pronounced dead at the hospital.

Mr. Sothers, a pack-a-day smoker for thirty-two years, had vowed to quit smoking four months earlier. The doctors thought his heavy cigarette smoking was a big contributing factor in his death.

Formerly a mathematics professor at Norfolk State University, just a month ago he had received the Professor of the Year award. His colleagues, faculty members, students, and friends flooded the church and gravesite to give their condolences.

Out of his two sons and daughter, Tory, who was at the store when he'd received the news and rushed over to the hospital, took the loss of their father the worst. Since his father's passing, except for checking on his mother every morning, all he did was lay in bed or sleep all day. When I tried talking to him, he would tell me he wanted to be left alone. Because I was his wife and best friend, I didn't take it personally. People grieve in different ways.

Tory's boss, Irvin, and his wife had also attended the funeral. Yvette, Leah, Tara, and their husbands all came to express their condolences to Tory and his family. Besides Tara, none of us had experienced the pain of losing a parent.

The gracious ladies from the church handled the repast, which took place in the basement of the church. They prepared Mr. Sothers' favorite dishes including roast beef with potatoes and carrots, fried chicken, and ham biscuits.

"He's with the Savior now," Evelyn whispered in my ear as she leaned in to give me a hug.

"Yes, ma'am, he is." I didn't know what to say to truly comfort her.

"Hold on tight to Tory. He will need you. I'm worried about him. I don't like the lost look in his eyes."

"I will be right by his side," I declared, reassuring her. "I know we can get through this. Losing a parent is something I can't even imagine. Leah and I are so close to my parents. That's probably why Tory looks so lost and empty. To be honest, I wouldn't know what to do either."

"Nya, that boy is lucky to have you."

"Thank you, Mrs. Sothers. I'm going to go check on him."

I found Tory sitting alone in a corner, his head down. "Would you like for me to fix you a plate?"

I asked, rubbing his shoulder. He hadn't eaten in days.

He shook his head. "No, I'm not hungry."

"Are you sure? The ladies made you and your daddy's favorite, roast beef."

"I'm sure." He nodded.

"What about a drink of sweet tea?" I showed him my glass with a wedge of lemon.

"No, I'm good."

"All right." I gave him a small peck on the forehead.

Three hours later, as people were starting to leave, Tory was still sitting in the same spot.

Chapter 8

Three weeks later, at the reading of the will, we learned that Mr. Sothers had left each of his children $125,000 from his insurance policy. Along with retirement benefits, their house being paid off, and numerous insurance policies, Tory's mother was going to be well taken care of.

Sitting at the attorney's office, Tory looked like a zombie. He'd fallen into severe depression, refusing to carry on with any of his daily activities and hadn't shaved and showered in days. Sleep was one of his few comforts. He was either trying to sleep his sorrows away, or trying to forget about the death of his father. Waking up was hard for him to do. He tossed and turned all morning, and when he finally got out of bed, it was to grab a bottle of Absolut vodka, Beefeater gin, or Bacardi rum.

At night, he'd tell me countless stories about his father. My favorite was the Labor Day cookout. Tory was a seven-year-old prankster, Steven was twelve, and Anne was eleven. While Steven was riding his bike, Tory went inside to tell his parents, grandparents, aunts, and uncles that Steven was hit by a car, and, of course, all the family members ran outside to see how Steven was.

"Gotcha!" Tory chuckled.

His father grabbed his behind and beat the hell out of him for pulling a stunt like that. In one moment, Tory and I would be laughing about these stories, and the next moment, his head would be in my lap crying.

His mother was very worried about him. I tried to encourage her and reassure her that Tory would snap out of it, but honestly, who knew how long he was going to continue on that way? I was going to be patient for as long as it took, but I didn't know what to do or what words to say to him to ease his pain and help him through it.

Chapter 9

Rome and I kept postponing the grand opening of the restaurant, Thai Temple, for as long as we could, thinking Tory would soon snap out of his depression. But, unlike Tory, the restaurant was Rome's only source of income, so I understood when Rome said he couldn't continue to wait on him. Not to mention, the rent on the property was due in a week, and I wasn't about to pay another month's rent on my own. I had to take money from Tory's inheritance to pay the last two months. I didn't want to keep dipping into the inheritance, so we needed to start generating money as soon as possible.

Tonight was the grand opening. Meanwhile, Tory was getting worse. Today, he'd doubled his usual intake of rum, gin, and vodka, along with a case of Coronas. I came home from work to find a bunch of limes and empty bottles sprawled over the island in the kitchen. Tory was in his boxers in the living room watching home movies. The stench of alcohol was now a regular feature in my home. I decided not to fuss about the mess in the kitchen and apply my energy to getting him out of the house.

"Let's go to the restaurant and stay for a little while. Rome would love to see you there. He needs your support. This is both of your dreams come true," I proposed, putting a dab of Carmex on my lips.

Tory yawned. "I don't feel like it. I'm going to sleep."

"What am I supposed to tell Rome?"

"Good luck." He shrugged his shoulders and headed toward the staircase.

Although Tory chose to stay home and wallow in sorrow, I decided to come out and show my support.

The grand opening of the restaurant was a huge success. The dining room was packed with customers, and we even had a waiting list. The money spent on promotions definitely paid off. I also helped to drum up buzz about the place by word of mouth—telling my coworkers, the dry cleaning lady, patients, and anyone else who would listen.

Wearing a sexy black pencil dress and red stiletto heels, I walked to the bar with style and confidence.

"Nya!" a voice called out.

I turned to see Rome walking toward me. "Hey, Rome," I said, admiring his grey suit. "You look great. The ladies are going to be all over you tonight."

"Thanks. I already got a few offers. Where's Tory?"

"He couldn't make it. He's still having a hard time dealing with the loss of his father. I know it's difficult for anyone to overcome the loss of a parent, but I'm hoping he'll recover from his depression soon. When you can, please call him and give him some words of encouragement."

"Since the funeral, I've called and left several voice mails, but he hasn't returned any of my calls. I know he's going through a rough time. I remember, from high school, how close him and his dad were. I'll continue to call and leave messages. Hopefully he'll call me back one of these days."

"Thanks. I appreciate it. This is a good turn-out," I said, looking around and changing the conversation.

"Yes, it is, which is fantastic for business. In the meantime, I don't mind playing host for the night, but my girlfriend Adriana is the jealous type and doesn't like the extra attention I'm getting." Rome cast his eyes in Adriana's direction.

"For your sake, don't act up," I teased, giggling.

"Well, enjoy yourself, Nya. I don't know if you're expecting any company for dinner, but the food is on the house, of course." Rome smiled at Adriana, who didn't look too happy sitting in a corner by herself.

"Thank you." I gave him a hug.

I knew Adriana wasn't worried about me. From the day we met, she and I had made a pact to keep an eye on each other's man if either one of us wasn't around, since we knew both of them would be spending a lot of time here constantly greeting customers.

As I headed to my reserved table, I noticed Yvette and Tara were already here.

"Thanks for coming." I hugged both of them.

Since her mother-in-law had made a permanent indentation in her couch, Yvette was ecstatic about getting out of the house. Leah and Tara were always going out, so they were accustomed to these events.

"Sorry I'm late," Leah butted in. She sat down at the table. "I couldn't find my MAC 'fix a face.' Besides, I couldn't pass up free food."

"The place looks wonderful," Yvette said.

"I agree." Tara raised her glass of Merlot.

"Hey, Christie," I said to our waiter when she came to our table. "This is my sister Leah and my two friends, Tara and Yvette."

"Nice to meet you," they said in unison.

I hadn't planned on it, but Tory's absence forced me to play an active role in the restaurant. Rome and I immediately liked Christie when she interviewed with us. She was young, charming, and energetic.

I'd even suggested to Rome that he let me handle the accounting. How hard could it be? Take money in with cash and credit card, make the bank deposits, do payroll and pay invoices out. As long as I stayed on top of things, I wouldn't have any problems.

"Likewise." Christie smiled. "Now what can I get you ladies to drink?" she asked eagerly.

"Shirley Temple for me with three cherries please," I told her.

"I'll have an apple martini," Leah said.

"I'm still working on the glass of red wine I picked up at the bar, so I'll just have a glass of water," Yvette explained.

"Let me get your drinks, and I'll be right back."

"Thank you," I responded.

Leah looked around our table. "Where are the menus?"

"The cooks are preparing seven different meals for us to sample. I figured it would be fun to try different dishes."

"So what's going on with Tory?" Tara asked.

"Besides becoming a drunk, he's fine," I shot back, crossing my arms.

"It's only been three months," Yvette said. "Give him some more time."

"I'm trying to, but it's hard. Yes, I understand he's dealing with the loss of his father, but I despise the way he's dealing with it by drinking himself to death. It's hard not to resent him since he knows I have a zero tolerance for anyone who abuses alcohol. It shouldn't be used as a form of escaping your problems or refusing to face your fears. The rate the man is going, he could potentially be at risk for liver damage."

"Maybe he needs to see a psychiatrist." Tara took another sip of her wine. "Y'all made me go, and I turned out just fine."

"I'm one step ahead of you. I already mentioned the idea to him."

"And what did he say?"

"He said no. I'm getting frustrated, Leah, because I can't have a conversation with him without an alcohol bottle in his hand. It's almost as if he's given up his will to live. He doesn't want to talk to anyone, including his mother."

Yvette gently grabbed my hand. "You know we're here for you."

"Tory is just going through a hard time right now," Tara added. "He's a good man."

Leah glanced at the table next to us. "He'll snap out of it."

"Thank you." I breathed a small sigh of relief, hoping things would get better for Tory and me.

"What dishes did you order?" Leah asked.

"It's a surprise. So what's been going on with everyone? I haven't had much time to catch up with any of you lately."

"I hate my mother-in-law. She's taking over my house. Jarvis is oblivious to all of it. If he even thinks I upset his precious mother, he gets mad with me. It's as if I'm competing for my own husband's attention." Yvette sighed. She looked as if a weight had been lifted off her shoulders, revealing that bit of information. "But tonight is about the opening of the restaurant, so I don't want to talk about *her* all night. On a lighter note, the women's shelter is doing great." She smiled. "I just got a few retail stores to donate new, sophisticated work clothes for the women who have interviews coming up."

"Nelson is getting frustrated with me because I won't set a date for the wedding. To be honest, I still want to have my fun. Settling down with children and suburban life doesn't interest me right now. Eventually, I'll settle down but not anytime soon. Oh! And he wants me to pick up more hours at my job. I can barely stand working my regular hours, and he wants me to pick up more?" Leah ran her fingers through her hair. "Six months ago, he relieved me of my second job. It was just in time too. It was beginning to cut into my going-out time. Now he keeps telling me he's tired of bailing me out financially, that I need to get my bills and money in order. Okay, so I spend a lot of money on clothes, shoes, and makeup. That's what it takes to be the hottest thing when I walk into the club. I refuse to give up my throne to some girl looking like she got her clothes from last year's clearance rack. I love having all the guys drool over me and how the women envy me."

"I don't envy you."

"Nya, you're my sister. You don't count."

"I'm going to ignore that last comment. Nelson is right about the finances though. You need to get it together."

"As far as going out, that's the way Nelson met you, so he needs to be patient," Tara added.

"I agree to a certain extent." Yvette looked at me and nodded. "Leah, if you really want to get married, you have to be willing to settle down. But that doesn't necessarily mean you have to lose your identity in the process. Obviously you're not ready for the married life and all the responsibility that comes with it. At least, you didn't have a baby and discovered you weren't ready—after the fact."

"Why can't you try to save at least two hundred dollars a month? Take a baby step at least. Your goal should be five hundred dollars, for the amount of money you make."

Leah shrugged her shoulders. "Things add up, and before I know it, my whole check is gone. I lay in bed at night wondering, 'What the hell did I buy?'"

I was starting to get annoyed with the conversation. "Are you going to save or not?"

"I'm not going to commit to something when I'm not sure of what I'm going to do yet."

"It's your choice to make, but when you're broke, don't complain about it."

"Have you noticed you're getting bags under your eyes?"

"Ha! Ha! Typical Leah! When you don't get what you want, you just *have* to point at stuff about me."

"Whatever. I don't complain about not having money to you, anyway, since you made it clear I can't borrow money from you anymore. Besides, Mommy and Daddy still bail me out every time."

"Borrowing is when you give money back. You take money and never give it back."

"Stop talking," Leah hissed. "You're beginning to give me a tension headache."

"Well, that's about enough of you two," Tara cut in. "The dealership has slowed down a lot, as far as sales. I'm glad I made the decision to become a finance manager. This way, my salary is guaranteed. Rob and I are doing fine. To be honest, I miss going out as much as I used to, but on the other hand, I have a man who truly cherishes me and accepts me for who I am. Last year, when he caught me out there with that DJ guy—hmm, I can't remember his name—my man forgave me and still married me. And, today, we are better than ever."

Tara knew how much Leah loved getting under my skin. My parents were pure enablers for Leah. Since I was the oldest, they didn't dare do the same thing for me because they'd always expected more from me. Leah had always had it so easy.

I smiled. "That's love, all right."

"Ladies, here are your drinks," Christie announced as she distributed the orders. "I am so sorry for the delay. Your entrees will be out in just a couple of minutes."

"Thank you," I told her.

That night, the four of us talked, ate, and laughed for hours. It was good to get out and spend time with my girls. Leaving those medical scrubs at home and getting dressed up made me feel great too. I needed to have some sort of outlet from Tory.

While driving home, I wondered if I was becoming depressed myself. A few minutes later, I found my husband laid out on the lawn next to his Range Rover.

After parking his truck in the garage, I tried desperately to wake him up, but he was too drunk to move on his own. It took me almost an hour to get him in the house and upstairs in the bed.

Chapter 10

"Nya, I just bought that bottle of rum yesterday. Why did you throw it away?" Tory barked at me while I was eating a bowl of hot grits.

"You mean, pour it down the kitchen sink drain," I corrected him.

"I will just buy more. Besides, I need it to get through," he pleaded, trying to convince me.

I took a sip of apple juice. "To get through what?"

"You know what . . . don't play games with me."

"Tory, what you need is a counselor to help you cope with the loss of your father."

"I don't need a damn shrink telling me how to feel and giving me pills to make me feel like a zombie."

"Too late. You already act like one. Let's go, please. I can even invite your mother, Anne, and Steven. Everyone is hurting. I can make an appointment for today, baby." I moved closer to him and rubbed his hand.

"You have your father. He's alive and well. I don' have my father. While he was having a heart attack, I was at the store picking up some damn sprinkles and ice cream for you. My cell phone reception is horrible in Farm Fresh. My mom said she called at least six times before she could get through."

"What are you trying to say?"

"I'm just saying, maybe if I wasn't getting junk food for you, maybe I could have saved my father," Tory slurred. "Who knows? I could have gotten him to the hospital faster than the ambulance." He took a big swig of a beer.

"Are you blaming me?"

"Yes. My father is gone, but you still got those sprinkles," he screamed. "By the way, you haven't touched them yet!"

"If you want to blame rainbow sprinkles and chocolate chip cookie dough ice cream on you becoming a drunk, go right ahead. You're right. My father is here. I'm grateful for that. No, I don't know how you feel. I couldn't imagine the hurt and pain. Instead of blaming me, why can't we get through this together? I'm trying to help you. I'm your best friend and, above all, your wife. Let me be there for you and get you the help you need."

"No. For the last time, I'm not going to see a psychiatrist. This conversation is over," he said before storming up the stairs.

After drying my tears, I headed to the hospital for work. I knew my eyes looked puffy. Plus, I had bags under them because of all the stress and lack of sleep. Lately, I couldn't get rest without taking a sleeping sedative. Most nights, I lay awake worrying about Tory and how I could get him to stop drinking.

On the way to work, I tried to relax and listen to a CD, *The Evolution of Robin Thicke*.

With a hefty salary increase and becoming a nurse practitioner, I wasn't required to be on the hospital floor as much. Still, what I loved the most was the time with the patients. Taking a quick glance on the medical chart, I saw that my first patient of the day was Kathleen Palmer, age twenty-four, who'd delivered a six-pound baby girl named Abigal, her first child.

I knocked on her door and went to the sink to wash my hands. "Good morning. I'm Nya, and I'll be your nurse for the next shift. How are you and baby Abigal doing?"

"Hi. Nice to meet you. I'm doing okay. The pediatrician just finished giving my little angel an examination." Kathleen doted on her daughter in the rolling hospital crib.

"Are you having any pain?" I inquired, taking her vital signs.

"Yes, but I took the ibuprofen."

"How long ago did you take it?"

"About an hour ago."

I started putting her updated vital signs in the computer. "Your baby is beautiful."

"Thank you. She looks like her father today. Maybe tomorrow she'll look like me." She giggled.

I leaned in to see her baby. "Well, she definitely has your lips, nose, and fingers."

"Yeah, she does. I carried her for nine months. Abby should have some of my features."

"Can I get you anything?" I asked, walking over to wash my hands again.

"No, I'm fine for now. My parents are here. They went to Starbucks for me. I can't wait to drink a mocha latte. I cut out caffeine throughout the whole pregnancy."

I smiled. "You certainly were disciplined. I probably would have cheated here and there."

The phone rang. As Kathleen talked on the phone, the baby began crying.

I changed her diaper and bundled her back up into her blanket. Once Kathleen hung up, tears began to stream down her face.

"Are you all right?"

"No, it was my husband on the phone. Three months ago, he was deployed to Iraq. It's hard with him being out there. I'm constantly worrying about him being injured or possibly coming back in a body bag. So many nights, I stay up wondering when next I'd hear from him. Now the baby is here, and it's like I'm a single mother. Not to mention, two years ago, we bought our first home in Chesapeake, so I have to take care of the bills and house by myself.

"I remember both of us were so excited to move into our first home. The only thing I cared about was decorating it. I spared no expense fixing up my baby's room with a custom-made crib. I was running up credit cards to the tune of fifteen thousand dollars, buying everything and anything I felt the house needed. That's when the bills started piling up. It also didn't help that we got an adjustable rate mortgage, which had ballooned. We were barely making our payment of eleven hundred dollars a month, and it has jumped to seventeen hundred dollars a month now. With my husband gone, I've had to deal with everything by myself." Kathleen was now sobbing.

I handed her a box of Kleenex tissues. "Did you try to refinance?"

"Yes, I did. The refinance payment would be fixed at sixteen hundred dollars a month, and I can't afford to have a fixed mortgage at that price. I'm better off with what we have now and waiting for it to go back down. With two car payments, food, utilities, the high price of gas, and now the baby's diapers and formula, I don't know how I'll get by. I've been using our credit cards just to survive. Now, we're all tapped out. No company will give me another credit card. We're already two months behind in the mortgage and will soon be facing foreclosure. My daughter may not have a house to grow up in." She continued to cry.

"I used to work at a bank called BankFIRST. Recently, they set up a program to work with homeowners on a payment they can afford." I jotted down a name and number on a piece of paper. "Here is a number I want you to call. Her name is Ruth Stein."

"Thank you so much," she said as I handed her the paper.

"You're welcome. While you're waiting for Starbucks, it's time for Abigal's feeding. Do you want to practice getting her latched on?"

"Yes, the sooner the better." Kathleen smiled. "She did well last night."

Chapter 11

I had the day off and the house all to myself. Tory had left early that morning without saying a word to me. We had gotten into an argument last night because I'd asked him when he planned on going back to work. Thankfully, Irvin was being patient with him, as far as giving him more time off to grieve. To me, though, it didn't seem like he was grieving anymore, just drinking. It was obvious he hated it when I complained about his excessive drinking, but it was also obvious he didn't plan on stopping anytime soon. Now, he was hiding alcohol bottles all through the house. While he was asleep, I searched everywhere to find them and pour them down the drain.

There was a strong knock at the door.

When Tory was on the loose and there was a knock at the door, I couldn't help but imagine the police at my door informing me he killed himself or someone else while driving drunk. We lived in Commonwealth Virginia, where the state doesn't take too kindly to drunk drivers. When talking to Tory about the dangers of drunk driving, it went in one ear and out the other. At times, I wondered why I even bothered. Then I'd remember the man I fell in love with and answered my own question. I refused to give up on him and our marriage and planned to stick it out.

I opened the front door just in time to see Leah waving good-bye to Nelson. "What do you want?"

"I need your help."

"The answer is no. Why did Nelson just drop you off here?" I quickly turned toward the living room, and Leah was on my tracks.

"Last night, my car got repossessed. Nelson was still working his shift at the restaurant when it happened. I lied to him this morning and told him I had dropped it off at the shop for a tune-up. It just so happens that today is my only day off this week."

"This is my day off too."

"Let me finish! I told Nelson you would drive me back to the dealership to pick the car up," she stated matter-of-factly.

"I'm not helping you, Leah. I don't need this today. I'm tired, and I need to rest. I just pulled a sixteen-hour shift and then had to do payroll and pay bills for the restaurant."

"Please? No one else will help me. If Nelson finds out, I'll have to hear his mouth. Mommy and Daddy said a month ago they weren't going to help me anymore. I think they meant it this time."

"How many months are you behind?"

"Four months. I spoke to the credit company, and they told me if I paid twenty-one hundred dollars today, I can get the car back."

"Why didn't you keep the Montero Sport I bought for you? Not having to make monthly payments is the way to go."

"The Montero Sport got old, and the two-door silver BMW 330i became more appealing."

"Your priorities are all messed up," I replied, shrugging my shoulders and sitting down on the couch in the living room.

"Maybe I have an addiction to shopping," Leah said nonchalantly.

"Leah, shut up. You are not starring in a Lifetime movie."

"I will help you on one condition," I said reluctantly, shaking my head. Yes, I admit I was definitely an enabler for her, but she was my sister. She had to have something to ride in.

"You have to pay me back within six months. Three hundred fifty dollars a month to me shouldn't be hard. I'm going to make a contract and get it notarized at the bank. After you sign it, we'll go get your vehicle. Soon, we will be facing our thirties. Do you really want to have nothing to show for working but your clothes, shoes, and makeup?"

"Nya, I'm going to do better."

"Credit and having your *own* stability should be important to you."

Leah nodded her head. "You're right."

"When we get back, I'm going to take a nap." I started putting on a pair of sneakers.

Thankfully, Leah didn't have any credit card debt, since Nelson made it a habit to give her pre-paid Visa cards.

Chapter 12

It was an unusually warm day for February. Before leaving for work, I opened most of the windows, so fresh air could circulate throughout the house.

I had a long work schedule that would consist of me being in and out of hospital meetings all day. Due to the economy, the hospital administrators were obligated to cut back on annual salary increases. Grateful that we wouldn't be losing our current salaries, I took it in stride. The most we could get for the next year was four percent, which was still better than nothing.

I was especially thankful that Tory and I had agreed to a fixed mortgage rate when we'd purchased our home. I couldn't count on my fingers how many of my coworkers were losing their homes because of adjustable rate mortgages. If times got real rough, I had the stash of money Brennon gave me. Other than what I'd contributed to Yvette's shelter, I hadn't touched it. It was sitting quietly in a safety deposit box collecting dust. To this day, I hadn't told a soul about that.

On my way home from work, I was in the mood for a mango Frutista Freeze from Taco Bell. Soon I regretted pulling up in the drive-thru because the person in front of me took twenty-five minutes with their order. As I waited impatiently, I wondered if I was the only person this happened to.

On my way home, I decided I didn't want to fight with Tory this evening. I decided to casually speak to him, take a shower, eat leftovers, try to sort through the mail, and go to sleep earlier than usual.

"Hey," he greeted me at the door when I walked in, Billie Holiday playing in the background.

"Hi," I responded.

"Follow me," he whispered in my ear, motioning with his finger.

Candles were lit everywhere in the dining room. He had two placemats set on the table along with a card addressed to me. The front of the card read: *I'm sorry*. When I opened it, *Will you forgive me?* was handwritten in it.

"Nya, I know it's been hard putting up with me these last few months, and I'm very sorry for the way I've been treating you."

"Of course, I forgive you. I love you." I gave him a small peck on his lips and a long hug. I smelled a hint of whisky on his breath.

"Sit down."

"What are we eating tonight?"

" It's your favorite, the Tour of Italy, for you, and fettuccine Alfredo for me from Olive Garden. I've been keeping it warm in the oven." Tory took off my heels and rubbed my feet, which relaxed me.

Dinner was perfect. Tory even remembered to substitute the chicken parmesan for grilled chicken with marinara sauce and mozzarella cheese just the way I liked it. He racked up twenty brownie points for that. It was the little things about our relationship that mattered the most to me.

"I'm full. Thank you for dinner, baby. It was lovely." I giggled, rubbing my stomach.

"That's not all."

"Really?"

"For dessert, I bought you a slice of tiramisu. I'll go get it from the refrigerator."

Tory cut off a small spoonful of the tiramisu and fed it to me. He began dabbing the mascarpone cream cheese on my neck and licking it off. We began kissing. We had definitely been missing each other.

He unbuttoned my medical shirt then took off my wifebeater and bra. He gently laced my right nipple with the sweet cream cheese and sucked it off. This was just what I needed—my husband to kiss me, caress me, lick me, suck me, and most of all, fuck me. He squeezed my breasts and slowly licked his way down into my inner thighs. I moaned as he kissed his way toward my pussy.

He took off his clothes and led me to the Jacuzzi. It was in the corner of the backyard and dark outside, so no one could see what we were doing. At this moment, I didn't care if anyone saw. I wanted Tory inside of me. Now.

The water was warm to the touch. Tory and I began kissing again, while my hand rubbed his dick. Then he picked me up and, with my ass hanging over the edge of the Jacuzzi, opened my legs wide and started sucking my clit, licking it up and down. Me coming in his mouth was going to be the ultimate dessert for me.

Suddenly, Tory stopped, got out of the Jacuzzi, and pulled me out. Not being able to make it to the bedroom, we ended up on the staircase.

"I want you to feel me," he cooed in my ear. "It's been too long." He slid his dick inside my moist pussy.

I was in total ecstasy as he kept giving me deep, long strokes. Just as I was about to come, he stopped.

"Tory!" I called out and shook the hell out of him. Damn it; he fell asleep in the middle of us having sex. Pissed off, I left him snoring right on the staircase.

I went downstairs to clear off the dining room table, wash the dishes, turn off the CD player, and finish eating that slice of tiramisu. I finished just in time to tune in to reruns of *Will and Grace*.

Chapter 13

Since our unforgettable night of apologizing about a month ago, things between Tory and I had worsened. To be spiteful, Tory was now leaving empty bottles in the places where he used to hide full bottles. Every morning before I left for work, all I would see was his lips wrapped around a bottle. His lips needed to be on me, damn it.

Every other day, I searched his truck and all throughout the house for alcohol. He had become more resentful toward me and wasn't saying much at all. Last Saturday, he slept for seventeen hours. Things didn't seem to be turning around for the better, and getting our relationship back to the way to the way it was before his father died seemed like an unreachable goal at this point.

In our guest room, Tory had his father's clothes all over the bed, and his shoes piled in the corner next to the window.

I understood that he felt closer to his father by having most of his clothes, so trying to be considerate and preserve the items, I bought storage bins to put them in and placed them in the attic.

This morning as I was preparing for work, he came in our bedroom and went ballistic, saying that I don't care about his feelings or his father.

My boss stopped me in the hallway. "Nya, may I have a word with you?"

"Yes."

She led the way into her office and closed the door. "Please have a seat. How are you doing?"

I grabbed a chair to sit. "Hmm. I'm all right."

"Well, to be honest, I'm concerned about you."

"How so?"

"Nya, you look tired, worried, and upset most of the time. It's as if something is troubling you. Don't get me wrong, you still do your job, a damn good job of giving quality care to our patients. I'm more concerned about what's going on with you personally. Is everything okay at home? I hope you don't think I'm prying. I just want to make sure you're okay. You're one of the best nurses I have working for me, and I hope to keep it that way. If you need some time off or anything else, please don't hesitate to speak with me."

"Ms. Canthen, I appreciate the concern, but I'm all right. Thanks for the positive feedback about my performance."

"Call me *Jill*, please. Your parents raised you right, but I prefer *Jill*."

I laughed. "Okay, I will."

"If those sixteen hours shifts are getting too much for you, let me know. A change of pace isn't a bad alternative."

I stood to shake her hand. "Thanks." I walked out of her office feeling good that someone cared.

After examining my patients this morning, I had worked up quite an appetite.

"So what dish are we having today?" I asked Evita after entering the nurses' lounge. I was starving, and the lingering smell of her food down the hallway wasn't making it better.

Evita was from Puerto Rico and loved cooking us different dishes from there. She, Karen, Donna, and I got together every other month to learn and experience a new entrée. And I'd started looking forward to spending time with them. To be honest, I loved coming to work. It got me out of the house and motivated me to keep life going.

"It's a chicken dish," Karen answered, setting the table.

Karen and I had been working together for two years. Right now, she was going through a bitter divorce with her husband, Cole.

Seven months ago, one day after she'd had back surgery and was laid up in the hospital, he decided to end the marriage. What a jerk! After all of that, she still wanted him. Karen was too nice for her own good.

During the course of their six-year marriage, Cole did a lot of soul-searching to supposedly find himself. What he needed to do was find a job. He rarely worked and used going to school as an excuse to quit his job at Barnes and Noble. I truly think some people want to make going to school a lifetime career, instead of facing everyday realities such as the mortgage, light bill, and car insurance. Periodically, I reminded her that mean girls finish first.

Thankfully, they didn't have any children together. And since she made way more money than he ever would, Cole was under the delusion that he would get to keep the house and she'd have to continue to make the entire mortgage payments.

"Yes, ladies, it's chicken with red and green bell peppers and rice and beans cooked in olive oil. I used Goya Sofrito and Adobo seasoning on the chicken, dropped in diced garlic and onions in the beans, and put in a little bit of seasoned salt in the rice for added flavor. When the chicken was fully cooked, I added the peppers and oregano. Then, I let it simmer for fifteen minutes, and *listo*! Let's dig in."

"Sorry I was late. My patient almost broke her hip trying to get to the bathroom by herself. Mrs. Epstill refuses to use a bed pan." Donna shook her head after cracking open a can of Seagram's ginger ale.

Ever since graduating nursing school, she and I had been partners in crime. Donna was a hard worker and dedicated to her patients. Not to mention, she had a pretty good lucky streak. Within the past three years, she and her husband had won many radio contests and sweepstakes, which included free airfare, lavish hotels, and spending money. Having VIP status and rubbing elbows with Vivica Fox, Alicia Keys, and Kanye West at the BET Awards was one of her unforgettable trips as well as backstage access to the Grammy Awards. Donna was given the opportunity to meet Maroon 5, whose lead singer, Adam Levine, is a real cutie. She also met singer John Mayer, who was nothing but a gentleman to her.

I bit into the chicken. "This is good, Evita."

"Thank you." She nodded. "I buy most of my poultry and seasonings from Montego's. They sell everything fresh and organic, which makes the meal even better."

Donna said, "Nya, I appreciate you taking my shift last week. The kids had a ball at Disney World. It was hard to get them to leave the Magic Kingdom and try other parks."

"You're welcome." I smiled.

"Hey, ladies. Hello, Karen," David Smith greeted us.

"Hi," we replied in unison.

David was a pediatrician and was not only loved by the children, but the women as well. He was a male whore who loved them and left them. He loved to mix business with pleasure and continued to make the mistake of using the hospital for picking out his victims. In fact, a few nurses refused to work with him because of the way he treated them.

"Karen, call me later. Bye, ladies," he stated and walked away.

We all turned to look at Karen's blushing face.

"What?" she asked, her hands up.

"Nothing." I giggled and continued eating.

"I slept with him about a week ago," Karen declared. "It was good. Plus, it took him no time finding my G-spot. Since then, I haven't bothered to call him. He's used to women drooling over him. For the first time, I took it for what it was—sex."

"No wonder you have that huge smile on your face," Donna commented.

"Wow!" It surprised me to hear Karen talking like this.

"Will you see him again?" Evita asked.

"I don't think so."

Everyone started laughing.

"How is Tory doing these days? Is he getting any better?" Donna inquired, changing the subject.

"Ever since his father passed away, he's become depressed and has been drinking heavily. He won't get help, and I don't know what to do at this point," I explained, tears in my eyes.

"When I wake up, I cry. Before I go to sleep, I cry. Whenever I look at him or think about him, I want to cry because I feel so helpless."

"Give it time, Nya." Evita gave me a tissue. "He's going through a hard time right now."

"Donna and Evita, you two are older than me and been married longer than me. I just figured the older you get, the less problems you have," I said, shrugging my shoulders, fidgeting with a piece of red pepper. I'd suddenly lost my appetite.

"Do you want to leave him?" Karen asked.

"No, I don't, but I can't live like this forever. Besides arranging a nice candlelit dinner for me like a month ago, Tory treats me as if I don't exist. Alcohol and home movies of his father is what he cares about. Last week, he was up in the attic drunk, of course. He didn't bother to turn on the light and tripped over a box, almost breaking his nose."

"You will have problems till the day you die," Evita commented. "You and Tory need to work through them. It's the key to a good marriage."

"Don't leave him," Karen advised. "Maybe you can have a psychiatrist come to your home."

"Yeah," Donna added. "It's a good idea, since he doesn't want to leave the house."

"I will try it. I'm open to any new ideas. Thanks for listening to me."

"No problem." Karen squeezed my hand. "I'm always here for you."

"You're welcome," Donna added.

"I speak for everyone at this table. We all want to see you happy, Nya."

"Thank you, Evita." I nodded, feeling comforted, as I dried my tears.

Chapter 14

"Nya, is that you?" Tory asked after I dragged myself in the house after yet another long shift.

"Yes," I answered.

"Come here," he barked from the living room.

"Baby, what will it be tonight?" I asked sarcastically. "Some Captain Morgan, Johnny Walker, or Jose Cuervo? I bet they can all suck your dick better than I can!" I screeched, stampeding into the kitchen.

"I want to talk, and not about my drinking, please. I'm so tired of hearing your mouth." Tory came running after me.

"Talk about what?"

"Well, I've been going to Pop's gravesite a few times a week."

"Is it before or after you go the ABC store to pick up alcohol?"

"Right now, I don't need your lip. Will you just listen to me please?"

"My listening ears are on," I snapped, folding my arms.

"When I was at the gravesite, I received a revelation. I want us to have a baby."

"Is that the revelation?"

"Yes."

"We're not ready for a baby. No, what I meant to say is, *you're* not ready for a baby," I replied, shaking my head.

"I will change. I want to be a father. I waited for you to finish school and start your own career. It's time to start our family."

"No, I won't have a baby with you!" I shouted.

"Why?"

"Because I have a drunk for a husband! You can't even take the trash out or go get groceries, even though you're home all damn day. Last week, I asked you to put air in my tires. What did you tell me? You were too tired and you were going to take a nap. You couldn't even do that for me, but you want to have a baby? A child is a huge responsibility and you don't get nap breaks. You also can't just pick up and go when you want and be gone for as long as you desire, like you do now. Having a baby is a lifelong commitment. Tory, are you truly willing to give up the bottle to have a baby with me? That's what you'd have to do. You look me in the face and tell me you're going to stop your drinking. If so, we can get started and make a baby right now. I love you, but this marriage is spiraling out of control." I started crying, my head on his shoulders.

"I can't promise you I'll stop drinking. Besides, it's not that bad."

"So stop then, if it's not that bad."

"I can't," he shouted rubbing his temples together with his fingers, making me feel as if the mere sound of my voice was giving him an excruciating headache.

"Then I can't have a child with you. I refuse to have a baby and watch you pick up an alcohol bottle for yourself instead of a baby bottle for your child."

"I'm sorry." He tried to hold me close.

"Don't touch me. Until you get your ass together, I don't want to hear any more of your revelations. As far as I'm concerned, you're a drunk and you're selfish, which is a deadly combination." I pushed him away and stomped up the stairs.

Chapter 15

After taking a hot shower, I dozed off to sleep. When I awoke, I looked out the window to see if Tory's truck was in the driveway. Last night, he didn't bother coming home till three in the morning. The bars allowed him to drink in peace. I was wondering if tonight was going to be another repeat. The house phone rang.

"Hello?" I answered, groggy and hungry.

"She's driving me crazy," Yvette said.

"What did Grace do today?"

"Grace, the worst mother-in-law has turned my whole family against me. She's taking over my house. Even Smoky will go to her first, instead of me. I've had that cat since we were fifteen years old."

"I know." I nodded.

"If I suggest cooking anything for breakfast, lunch, or dinner, Jarvis has to ask his momma if it's all right with her."

"What? I know she's diabetic, but you can always fix her something separate. Or Grace can cook something herself."

"That's right. Grace uses her diabetes as a way to control the kitchen. Last week, Jarvis and I went to dinner. My parents watched the kids. She got upset that it was just the two of us going and got on Jarvis about how she's tired of having to limit what she can eat. Then she went on and on about how she wished she could go to a restaurant and eat anything she wanted. She pulled such a guilt trip on him, Jarvis decided to stay home with her. It's hard for him to see through her schemes. He's such a momma's boy, it's ridiculous!" She exclaimed into the phone.

"Did you talk to him about it?"

"Yes. He said that's his mother, and I make him feel as if he has to choose between her and me. Grace is miserable that her husband left her, but I can't blame him. She nags the hell out of me and she questions my every move. 'Where are you going? What are you doing? What time will you be back?' And she tries to control everything, like it's her house. I put out clothes for the kids to wear, and she will go right behind my back and put out clothes she wants them to wear. It's the little annoying things that are adding up."

"I don't think you're trying to make him choose. You just want a balance between the time he spends with his mother and you."

"Exactly."

"Why can't she move out into her own place?"

"She's stubborn. Jarvis' father offered her the house, which is already paid for, but she refused. She would rather control my house. On Sunday, she cooked dinner even though I had already cooked pork chops. Jarvis got mad with me because I wanted our family to eat what I made for dinner. He's starting to nitpick and point out everything I don't do that his mother does. What he needs to be looking at is everything I do for him and our family instead.

"No one is perfect."

"Something is going to have to give. I can't live like this any longer."

"Do you think she's jealous of you?"

"Well, Grace has mentioned a few times she regretted getting married too early and not going to college."

"That could very well be the reason why she's resentful toward you. You went to college, have a wonderful career, and established a beautiful family. She never worked a day in her life and didn't have many options but to be a stay-at-home mom. Most of all, you married her son. You know how mothers are when it comes to their baby boys."

"What should I do?"

"Stop talking to Jarvis, because it's a dead end. If I were you, I would make her life a living hell to the point where she wants to leave. That is your house, husband, and kids; remember that."

"You're right. Thanks, girl. I'm about finished folding clothes and will be heading to bed. Good night."

"Good night."

The next morning I found the truck sprawled over the lawn and Tory lying next to it. Again. I was amazed that he could make it all the way home but couldn't make it into the house. I parked the truck in the driveway and left him right where he was.

At seven thirty on the dot, I turned on the sprinklers. I laughed so hard seeing him run in the house cold and wet.

Chapter 16

Walking into my parents' house, I smelled chili simmering on the stove. Leah was supposed to be joining us as well. I was hoping she'd bring her three hundred and fifty dollar payment for this month instead of making me drive over to her house tomorrow.

"Hi, Daddy." I greeted him with a kiss on his left cheek. He was sitting on the couch watching the evening news on NBC.

"Hi, baby. How are things going with you and Tory?" he asked with a look of concern.

"I'm all right and working hard. My husband is still having a hard time with losing his father," I explained, twiddling my thumbs. Talking to Daddy about what was going on at home always made me nervous.

"Yes, indeed, it's a terrible thing to lose your father. I count my blessings every day that your granddaddy can still see another day. I know Tory's been hitting the bottle hard."

I was surprised Daddy knew Tory's dirty little secret. "How do you know?"

"Well, I saw him at the liquor store a couple of weeks back."

"Oh."

"Yep. He was pretty loaded up."

"Wow!"

"Let me say this. I'm only going to say it one time. If Tory puts his hands on you, one of us is going to die that night. Leah and you are all grown up, moved out, and got good jobs and all, but I'm still your daddy and y'all still my babies. Understand?"

"Yes, sir, I understand. Just so you know, he hasn't put his hands on me. He's not crazy or stupid. You see, Daddy, I believe a bowl of hot and steamy cream of wheat being thrown in his face should teach him a lesson if he ever puts his hands on me. That, along with a cast iron frying pan to the back of the head."

"I'm glad we understand each other." He chuckled and gave me a handshake.

"It's time to eat," Mommy interrupted.

"Hey, Mommy." I greeted her in the kitchen with a hug while Leah placed an envelope of money in my jacket. I didn't notice when she walked in the house. "Good girl." I nodded my head.

"You're welcome," she replied, rolling her eyes.

Not wasting any time, I fixed a bowl of chili piled with chopped sweet onions, extra cheddar cheese, a few drops of hot sauce, and a dollop of sour cream. On the side, Mommy made corn and raspberry muffins with fresh lemonade. She'd made the lemonade not too sweet, just the way I like it.

"So how's work at the hospital?" Mommy asked while I dried the last dish.

"Delivering babies is in my blood. I love it." I giggled.

"How's my son-in-law doing?"

"He's been drinking a lot, hasn't gone back to work, and is still in a rut. I don't know what to do." I placed the dish in the cabinet. "At times, I feel as if he can't stand the sight of me. Deep down, it hurts bad."

"Tory is hurting too." Mommy started rubbing my back.

"It's hard, Mom."

"Nya, you married him for better or worse. I know you've been struggling for a while now. Honey, just be a little more patient with him. Soon, he will stop living with the dead and come back to life. You can't relate to how he must feel to have lost his father. You and your sister are blessed to still have your father and I. You don't know how you will react when either of us passes on."

"You're right about that, Mommy." I began to think that, at times, I'd been a little insensitive, especially with my comments.

Seeing my parents lifted my spirits. It's funny. In my teens, I always thought they were a constant nag and roadblock to what I wanted. Now that I'd grown up, I realized they were the friends I never knew I had in my corner.

Chapter 17

Four pizzas and a bucket of hot and mild crispy chicken wings from Cal'z Pizza Place awaited me at the front door.

"Hi," the delivery guy stated after I opened the door. "The total is forty-seven dollars and twenty-three cents."

I handed him a fifty-dollar bill. "Keep the change. Thanks." I smiled as he gave me the food.

Two weeks ago, a drunk Tory walked into the sliding glass door and broke his nose. I thought seeing his friends would cheer him up. He was a little excited about Alex, an old college buddy, and his best friend Kevin coming over to watch the basketball playoffs with him. Even though I'd bought soda, Tory wasted no time bringing out the tequila, whisky, and Coronas from one of his many hiding places. Not to mention, Kevin pitched in and bought a bottle of Bacardi rum. Unfortunately, Neither Alex or Kevin was aware of Tory's recent drinking problem. I prayed that he wouldn't drink too much tonight, since I knew not drinking at all wasn't an option for him.

I fixed a plate with a slice of supreme pizza and a slice of cheese pizza sprinkled with red pepper flakes and parmesan cheese. I grabbed five wings with a saucer of blue cheese dressing and was heading upstairs to give the guys their space when Kevin and Tory stopped me in my tracks.

"Don't tell her," Alex pleaded with them. "She doesn't want to hear it."

"Don't tell me what? Now you got me interested," I said, egging Tory and Kevin on.

"Back in college, it was our junior year. It was an ordinary Wednesday night before finals in the dorm," Tory explained.

"Uh huh."

He continued, "To relieve some stress from his exams, Alex decided to go on the Internet."

Kevin nodded. "It's a haven for porn."

"Well, apparently he jerked off at his desk in front of the computer and fell asleep with his dick hanging out his pants and his hand smothered in cum."

"But Alex forgot one thing." Kevin had a sly smirk on his face.

I laughed. "What was that?"

"He forgot to lock his door!"

"We couldn't help but to take a picture." Kevin laughed as he held up the picture.

"I can't believe you knuckleheads still got that picture." Alex shook his head in embarrassment.

"Yep, we sure do," Tory said in between laughs.

Kevin was laughing so hard, he almost choked on his chicken wing. "This is pure classic comedy," he declared.

All of us were laughing. I laughed to the point where my stomach was hurting.

Afterward, I retreated to my room to enjoy my food and indulge in an ice-cold can of Fanta peach soda.

After watching the DVD *Under the Tuscan Sun* and three episodes of *Tyler Perry's House of Payne*, I was ready to dig into some more chicken wings. I was hoping the guys hadn't finished them all.

When I entered the kitchen, all I saw was empty bottles and beer cans scattered on the floor. And Kevin, Alex, and Tory were nowhere to be found. Suddenly, I heard a loud thump in the garage.

"What happened?" I pushed Kevin and Alex out of the way as they gawked at Tory lying at the bottom of the four stairs that led from the kitchen to the garage. Both looked drunk and reeked of alcohol.

Alex said, "Tory was supposed to be getting more alcohol for us. While getting up from the couch to head to the garage, he kept saying he couldn't breathe. I asked him if he was all right, and he said, 'Yeah.' The next thing you know, we heard a noise and we came to see if he was all right."

I leaned over Tory, and he wasn't moving at all.

"Oh shit! Is he dead?" Kevin asked, pacing the floor.

"Tory, can you hear me?" I shook him.

"What are we going to do?" Alex questioned, now panicking.

"One of you, grab the phone in the kitchen and call 9-1-1." I cradled Tory in my arms, praying he would wake up. I couldn't help but wonder if maybe he truly wanted to die. *I can't let him go like this*, I thought. I loved him with all my heart. Our lives weren't supposed to be this way.

Chapter 18

Seeing their good friend unconscious on a stretcher made Kevin and Alex sober up quick. While waiting for the doctor to give us an update on Tory's status, I poured my heart out to them, explaining how he had become an alcoholic and how hard it's been for him to cope with the loss of his father. Kevin felt horrible about bringing alcohol to the house. I told him not to feel guilty about it because he didn't know of Tory's addiction. I was hoping the two of them could talk some sense into Tory, if he came out of this okay.

I called Tory's brother and sister and told them what had happened. They immediately came to the hospital. Both of them preferred that I not call his mother, since she would be worried sick about him. Plus, they didn't want her out at this time of night.

"Mrs. Sothers?" the doctor called out. "I'm Dr. Saunders."

I got out of my seat, and Anne, Steven, Kevin, and Alex crowded around me. "How is he?"

"Your husband fell hard and bruised a few of his ribs. He passed out from alcohol poisoning. The amount of alcohol he drank tonight could have killed him. We pumped his stomach and were able to stabilize him. Does your husband drink often, Mrs. Sothers?"

"He used to be a social drinker. His father died some months back, and he's been drinking daily ever since."

"I strongly urge that you get him into a rehab center as soon as possible. I know of a few centers that I highly recommend. Alcoholism is a deadly disease and can potentially ruin the liver. We're treating him with fluids. I want to keep him here the next couple of days for further observation. When he wakes up and is able to talk, I'm ordering a psychological evaluation on him. You and the rest of his family must be patient and be available to him. He will need all the support he can get. I should know—I used to be an alcoholic. It's not an easy road to recovery, but Tory has got to want to get better." Dr. Saunders seemed proud to reveal his sobriety chip.

"Thank you, doctor."

Anne consoled me in her arms.

"I hope he gets better, Mrs. Sothers." Dr. Saunders handed me various brochures on treatment centers.

"You're far too young to be dealing with this," Anne whispered in my ear.

"That boy knows better than to be acting like this." Steven shook his head.

"Our father would be so disappointed in my little brother," Anne added.

"And kick his ass!"

"What can we do to help?" Kevin asked eagerly.

"Get every last empty bottle out of my house!"

Whether Tory liked it or not, I was going to save his life. He no longer had a choice or say in the matter.

I had taken my boss up on her offer to take some time off from work.

A week later, Tory was still in the hospital. After his psychiatric evaluation, the doctors determined that he was in a severe state of depression and was borderline suicidal. He refused to eat and was barely speaking to any of us. His mother was at his side every chance she had. I was afraid she'd die of a broken heart over her son.

Steven continued to look at Tory with some disgust, while Anne pitied him. Despite everything, they loved their baby brother and were willing to do whatever it took to help him get better and kick alcohol for the rest of his life.

Leah, Tara, Yvette, and I combed my house and found twenty empty alcohol bottles and fifteen unopened bottles. The sight of alcohol repulsed me. It had overtaken my husband and house. Now, I was on a mission to reclaim what belonged to me.

Even though the ambulance had rushed Tory to Chesapeake General Hospital instead of where I worked, the news had somehow found its way to my job anyway. Upon my return, I anticipated all the nosy folks getting all in my face, asking questions and wondering what had happened, acting like they really cared. I knew more than half of them would be asking for the sole purpose of having something to gossip about. It's true what they say: People love drama, especially when it's not their own.

I was thankful for my coworkers Evita, Karen, and Donna. They each called me once a day to make sure I was okay and to ask if I needed anything. Evita even dropped off some food for me on nights I stayed late at the hospital with Tory. That woman's cooking was delicious. She gave me something to look forward to whenever she'd call to tell me she had a plate ready for me.

Chapter 19

Evelyn was sitting in the right corner of the couch, tears pouring down her face, and two Kleenex tissues in her hand.

"Are you ready to do this?" I asked.

She nodded her head. "Yes, I think so."

Dr. Waters, a bald middle-aged man with a mustache that looked more like whiskers, looked around the room. "Is everyone here?"

Dr. Waters came highly recommended. He'd been a psychiatrist specializing in drug addiction for the last thirty years. And he participated with our health insurance, so they were footing the entire bill for his treatment.

Evelyn, Steven and his wife, Anne with her husband, Alex, Kevin, and I were in his office. Surprisingly, Alex and Kevin, Tory's two best buddies, looked extremely nervous.

My heart went out to Tory's mother. Since his accident, she'd worried herself so much, she'd been experiencing anxiety attacks. Mrs. Sothers should be enjoying her life. At her age, it was a shame and awful that she had to go through this. She had already experienced the loss of her husband and now she had to deal with her alcohol-addicted son.

I nodded. "Everyone is here."

"I want to start off by thanking each and every one of you for attending this meeting. It takes a lot of courage to help someone you love. Tory is heading down a road of darkness, despair, and possible death. We're here today to do an intervention and encourage him to go for treatment and get some help. In treatment, he'll learn how to cope with the loss of his father without alcohol consumption. The nurse is wheeling him down to my office as we speak."

"Hey. What's everyone doing here? Why are Alex and Kevin here?" Tory inquired as he entered the office. Dressed in a hospital gown, robe, and slippers, he looked tired and somewhat pale.

"We're here to help you," Kevin announced.

"Are you now?" Tory asked, his eyes fixated on Dr. Waters.

"I'm Dr.—"

Tory cut him off. "Help with what? There's nothing wrong with me," he barked.

"Son, let the doctor finish."

"Tory, I'm Dr. Waters, and we're all here today because we care about you."

"Man, you don't even know me!"

"Dr. Waters cares about all of his patients. He along with everyone in this room wants you to go to treatment for alcohol. Tory, I love you, but you're a drunk. Alcohol is killing you and our marriage. I can't live like this anymore. Our lives weren't supposed to play out like this." Now, I definitely needed a few Kleenex tissues because the tears were spilling down my face.

"Tory, I want you to be the man, brother, husband, and father that you were meant to be. I know you miss your father; we all do. But you have got to give up the booze," Evelyn told him.

"If I don't?"

"I'm changing the locks at your house tonight," Steven responded. "No woman should have to put up with your drunken binges and rants. Nya deserves better than that." He stood to his feet. "And don't you even think about coming near my momma! You don't know how many nights I've stayed up with her worried sick about you while you laying up in your hospital bed because you're not man enough to deal with Pop's death and had to resort to drinking. Nya told me about your drunk driving too. Don't you know it's a crime to drink and drive? I never imagined my little brother would be stupid and selfish enough to put himself and others at risk like that. You could kill somebody driving drunk. You don't want to do something about your problem? Fine. But, just so you know, I don't visit people in prison."

I never expected Steven to explode the way he did.

"She's my momma too!" Tory yelled at the top of his lungs. "It seems everybody has gone on with their lives and forgot about Pops, except me. No one cares."

Anne said, "Just because we're not drinking ourselves into an early grave doesn't mean we don't miss Dad. We all miss him, but you got to do better than this. Mom and Pops raised you better than this. Go get the treatment."

Tory shook his head. "No, I'm not going anywhere."

"Get the help. I'll come visit you and do whatever it takes for you to get better. It will save your life. Truth be told, I haven't had one drink since we found you in the garage. I thought you were dead. It scared the shit out of me." Kevin looked at Tory's mom. "Excuse me for cursing, Mrs. Sothers."

Alex joined in, "I can count on one hand who my true friends are. Tory, you're one of them. You can't go out like this. You're destroying yourself. I don't want to have to explain to my kids why they can't go to your house and visit anymore. You're their godfather. They should be spending more time with you. Please . . . We're all here today because we love you. We want to see you get better."

"How long is the treatment?" Tory asked.

Dr. Waters responded, "It will be a ninety-day treatment. If you agree, we leave tonight on a plane headed toward Richmond. There's a nice rehabilitation center on the outskirts of the city."

"All right, I'll go."

"You will?" I asked, excited at the prospect.

"If that's what I have to do to keep my friends and family, I don't have much of a choice then. Who else besides Kev and Alex is going to eat chicken wings with me during playoffs? Who else is going to fulfill my dreams as you do, Nya? Who's going to believe in me even when I don't believe in myself?" Tory turned toward his brother and sister. "Steven and Anne, who's going to get in my ass when I need it? Most of all, who's going to fix me the best jambalaya I've ever had than my momma?"

I hugged him. "I love you. This will be a fresh new start for you." This was one of the happiest moments of my life. I knew this would turn out well, which was why his bags were already packed.

Later that evening, Tory was released from the hospital. Everyone, including Dr. Waters, went to Evelyn's house for dinner and had a bowl of hot jambalaya. When saying farewell, I cried, but they were tears of joy, not sorrow.

Chapter 20

There was a knock at the door. I immediately ran to look through my peephole to see who it was.

A hysterical Yvette sprinted into the house, almost knocking me down in the process. "I parked my car on the next street over, Nya."

"What's going on? Why would you park your car over there when you can park in the driveway?"

I sipped on my ice-cold glass of Lipton Diet Green Tea. I normally didn't like diet drinks, but lately, my clothes started fitting a little bit too tight. I couldn't even get into my favorite pair of jeans. I had to start being more conscious of what I was putting into my body.

"Jarvis found out. He caught me in a lie. He's going to kill me."

"Found out what?"

"That I was having an affair."

I gasped, choking on the tea. "What?"

"Well, he has suspicions. I need you to cover for me. Tell him last night we went to the movies and saw the new Indiana Jones release. Here are the tickets stubs for the seven thirty showing. If he asks, after the movie, you and I went and grabbed sandwiches at Wawa. We don't have much time to talk. He's on his way over here right now."

"Wait. I don't understand. Why would I need to tell him this?"

"Because he's on the way over here. Right now!"

"But you don't have it in you to stray away from Jarvis."

Yvette simply put her head down. "Please . . . I'm begging you. Tell him I was with you. He's going to leave me if he finds out I lied to him. I can't lose him or my family," she said, running up the stairs. "I'm going to your closet to hide."

The doorbell rang, and was followed by two loud knocks on the door.

"Who is it?" I asked, forgetting to look through the peephole as I usually do before answering the door.

"Nya, it's me, Jarvis."

I opened the door. "Hi, Jarvis. Is everything all right with Yvette and the kids?" I asked, trying to play my role.

"Sorry to be barging in on you like this. Yeah, Yvette and my babies are fine. Can we talk?" Before I could even answer, Jarvis had made his way to my living room.

"Sure," I replied as I closed the door. I was praying that Yvette stayed put in the closet and didn't try to sneak and listen to whatever Jarvis had to say. I didn't want him to catch her here, because then he would really think something was up, and she would look even more guilty.

"I need to ask you something. Nya, I trust your word."

"Yes?"

"Last night, did you and Yvette catch a movie?"

"Yep, we sure did. We watched Harrison Ford starring in the new Indiana Jones movie. Afterward, I made the mistake of smothering onions on my panini from Wawa and paid the price of having agonizing heartburn."

"Thanks for letting me know." Jarvis let out a huge sigh of relief.

"You're welcome." I smiled.

"Things have been a little rocky between Yvette and me."

"You two are the exception to the rule and have been dating since we were all in junior high school. One thing I know for sure, Yvette and you love each other very much. Of course, there'll be bumps in the road and everyday life gets in the way, but whatever is going on, you two can work it out. I'll be right back," I informed him, running into the kitchen.

I came back and handed him a note.

"What's this?"

"It's a gift card to you and Yvette. This card guarantees that I will babysit for five nights. Love is in the air. Maybe you two can get away and spend more time together to iron out your problems."

"Good idea." Jarvis hugged me. "Thanks, Nya."

"You're welcome."

"By the way, how's Tory rehab treatment coming along?"

"He's good and making progress. Last weekend, I went to visit him. Tory is taking it one step at a time. It's all I can ask him to do right now."

"It's not the same without him. I miss us all hanging out, you know."

"I do too. We've all had some fun times together."

"Remember when Natalie fell in the pool and almost drowned? My man Tory saved the day by quickly grabbing her arm. I will always be grateful to him for that."

I nodded. "Yes, I remember."

Jarvis got up. "Well, I got a few things to take care of. Thanks again." And he headed to the door.

I peeped through the window to make sure he made it out of my driveway. After I saw him drive toward Greenbrier Parkway, I ran upstairs to find Yvette huddled in a corner in my closet.

"Is he still here?" she asked, silently crying.

"Jarvis is gone." I extended my left arm to help her out of the closet. As she continued to cry, I held her in my arms on the bed.

"I don't want anyone to judge me."

"Judge you for what? What's going on? We've been friends far too long now. Spill it."

"Nya, I did it."

"Did what?"

"I've been seeing someone else. Last night, we finally had sex. Why are you looking at me like that?"

"I don't know what to say. To be honest, I'm surprised. I never thought you'd cheat on Jarvis."

"Let's clarify this. Did you think I wouldn't have the nerve to cheat on Jarvis, or on anyone in general?"

"I didn't think you had it in you to cheat on anyone."

"He doesn't know what I'm capable of. No one does."

"How long has this been going on?" I asked, still dumbfounded by what she was telling me.

"Four months. His name is Wayne. He's got dark chocolate skin, sculpted muscles, and a sense of humor. He's always made me laugh. That's the best part of why I took such a liking to him."

"How'd you meet him?"

"At the gym. At first, it was strictly platonic. We would talk about the usual stuff, my husband, his wife, the kids, our careers. This was all around the time Jarvis and his mother were constantly harping on me about everything I did and didn't do. I got tired of all of it. Plus, him being up his momma's butt wasn't helping either. I felt I was losing him. Wayne became a shoulder to cry on, and made me feel accepted, just as Jarvis used to do. I missed that."

"What made Jarvis suspicious of Wayne?"

"I forgot my cell phone this morning. Natalie started playing with it and then handed it to him. Shortly after, I got a text from Wayne saying that he enjoyed last night and wanted to see me again. I didn't know what else to say but to tell him that I was out with you."

"Did you mention Wayne to him at all?"

"No, not at all. When Jarvis saw the text on my cell phone, I denied even knowing whose number it was and told him it must have been a wrong number. I don't have his number stored in my phone and I always erase my call history to make sure Wayne's number isn't on my phone."

"Not all men are idiots and stupid, Yvette. Deep down, Jarvis must still think something's going on. Hopefully, with me confirming we went out last night, he'll have all the reassurance he needs to move on from the situation. Look on the bright side of this, Jarvis felt highly threatened at the thought of you being with another man, so now maybe he'll start treating you better and realize it's only him and you in the marriage and take his mother out. She's been causing a lot of friction between the two of you. Now I see why his sister wasn't too quick to let Grace live in her house with her family. No one wants their home disrupted."

Yvette sighed. "You have a point."

"What about Wayne?"

"I ended things with him this afternoon. He said he understood and knows how much I love Jarvis. Plus, I'm sure he's not leaving his wife anytime soon. We both agreed it was a mistake and admitted we both acted on impulses. The feeling of having someone new to be physically intimate with is great. Hell, I still want him right now! Let's just say, Wayne knows how to work with his gym equipment." Yvette giggled. "Eventually that feeling of euphoria will go away. Last night was unexpected. I was enjoying myself. The movie was good. Then we indulged in strawberry shortcake together and shared almost an entire bottle of wine. Next thing I know, we're at the Marriott Hotel making out and fondling each other like a couple of teenagers. I wanted him so bad. Wayne made me feel desired and enjoyed my company. Afterward, I felt terrible and mainly disappointed in myself."

"Well, the fact you haven't been with any other man besides Jarvis doesn't help either. The curiosity probably got the best of you. You're human, Yvette. You made a mistake."

She nodded.

"Things are all right, now. Go get your husband. Don't ever tell him the truth. Men have a hard time getting over us giving their pussy away to someone else. It's a territorial thing."

"Believe me, you won't have to ever worry about me confessing the truth to him. I'm curious though—why did you go along with the lie?"

"I went along with it because I know you would do the same for me. Most of all, I love Jarvis. He's like a brother to me, even though, ultimately, my loyalty is with you."

"Okay. Thanks for sticking up for me today." Yvette gave me a hug.

"No problem."

"A weight has been lifted off my shoulders. The thought of losing Jarvis and my kids terrified me."

"You won't lose them. I know it's easier said than done, but try not to think about it. Focus on the future and start moving on from this."

Chapter 21

"Let me give you some gas money." I handed Tara a wrinkled twenty-dollar bill that was crammed in my pocket.

Gas prices were creeping up close to four dollars a gallon. Some of my patients were telling me about the really hard times they were going through, some of them pawning anything of value to pay for everyday living expenses.

Next to the mortgage payment, my biggest expense was gas, which was ruling everything right now. It took forty-five dollars to fill up my tank. I refused to go over that amount. Now, I thought about where I was going, how long it would take, and whether it was even necessary for me to go.

Tara had picked me up from the airport. I was supposed to have landed at eight, but there was a three-hour flight delay. It was now 11 p.m., and I was exhausted.

For training and conference purposes, I had flown to Chicago. The only thing I had truly looked forward to there was a restaurant called the Oven Grinder Company, where they made pizza potpies. It's a bowl, any size you choose, of mozzarella cheese, meat, and vegetables in a marinara sauce topped with fresh dough. My trip wouldn't have been complete without stepping foot into that restaurant, which was a local favorite with friendly and prompt service.

"Nya, please put your money away. It's no good to me."

"Tara, take the money. Gas is too high for you to be saying no."

"My word is final. But, speaking of high gas prices, we can't even give away a truck at the dealership these days. No one wants to come near those gas guzzlers."

Whenever Tara was upset about something, she'd start complaining about something else totally unrelated to what was really bothering her.

"Is something on your mind?" I asked, as I waited for the luggage to come my way.

"The anniversary of Mom's death is coming up soon. I miss her, that's all."

"I know you miss her. We all do. How's your father dealing with it?"

"Dad's fine. He's dating again. At first, I wasn't too enthused with the idea but I don't want him to be alone for the rest of his life either. I mean, that would be selfish of me."

"I disagree with you. If either one of my parents began dating after the other died, I wouldn't be too happy. To be honest, I might even sabotage the relationship. Yes, when it comes to my parents, I'm very selfish."

We both began giggling.

"Dad is more worried about me having another breakdown, but I told him I was fine. Do you remember we're all going to the gravesite on Saturday to put fresh flowers down?"

"I sure do."

Every month Tara puts fresh flowers on her mother's grave to help her cope with the loss.

Chapter 22

"Mrs. Sothers, you can come down off the scale now," the nurse told me. "You're at one hundred and forty-five pounds. It's sixteen pounds more than you were a year ago. Now, before you go into room two, I need to get a urine and blood sample."

"What? I don't understand how I've gained so much weight," I announced after giving her the samples she requested. Lately, I'd been eating less because I was working so much. This wasn't adding up.

"Maybe it's something you're taking. I shouldn't speculate. I will notate your medical chart for Dr. Hicks to speak with you about your weight concerns and the stomach pain you've been experiencing," she stated after taking my heart rate and blood pressure. She jotted down some notes in my chart.

"Thanks. The stomach pain feels more like a burning sensation."

***

About a half an hour later, there was a knock on the door.

"Come in," I announced.

"Nya, it's always a pleasure to see you. How's everything going? How's your husband Tory?" Dr. Hicks inquired, while washing her hands in the sink.

"I'm doing all right. Tory is still in the rehab center and finding other ways to cope with the loss of his father. I appreciate the referral to Dr. Waters. He has been a tremendous help in the recovery process for Tory."

As I was speaking of Tory, I couldn't help but daydream about what we did the last time I went to visit him. While the rest of the visitors were outside enjoying nature, Tory and I snuck away and decided to go in his room. A gentle touch on my arm led to me riding him in a chair. Damn, it was good.

"I was happy to help," Dr. Hicks snapped me back into the consultations room. "I've been seeing your family for thirty years now, three generations of women, your grandmother, mother, Leah, and yourself. Over the years, you all have been good to me. Now, let's talk about you." She sat in her chair and flipped through my medical chart.

"Yes, the stomach pain is becoming hard to deal with." I rubbed my stomach.

"The lab ran the tests I requested. Your urine is normal. There are no signs of problems in the urinary tract, but your blood test revealed that you have developed an ulcer. I'm leaning more toward a stress-induced one. It's no wonder, with all the worrying and stress put on you from Tory's drinking."

"Now that I think about it, Dr. Hicks, when I'm mad or worried, my stomach does hurt more."

"I'm going to write you a prescription for the ulcer. I want to see you back in ninety days."

"If the medicine doesn't work, will I need surgery?"

"Yes, but try not to think so far ahead. I recommend you take a few days off and reduce what's stressing you. With Tory in recovery, that's a positive thing for his and your health too."

"What about the weight gain?"

"I'm not sure. For the last eleven years, you've been on the same birth control. Have you been eating more?"

"No, actually I've been eating less because I've been working so much at the hospital and the restaurant."

"By the way, my husband took me there two weeks ago. It was the first time he ever had Thai food, and we truly enjoyed it." She smiled. "I recommended three of my girlfriends try the place out as well."

"Thank you. Business is booming, and I want it to stay that way. Despite the horrible economy, the restaurant is proving people will still pay to eat good food and keep coming back. In terms of my birth control, you're right, I've been on Ortho Tri-Cyclen for years now. I try not to miss a day taking those green pills."

"Those pills, I believe, are yellow not green. Honey, do you have a pack with you?"

"Yes, I do. Let me get them." I rummaged through my purse and handed her the pack of pills.

"Oh my!" Dr. Hicks sighed.

"What's wrong?"

"These are the wrong birth control pills. The pharmacy has been giving you Nortrel instead."

"What? With everything going on, I didn't even notice the label was different."

"Not only that, the Nortrel pack has the doctor's name on it. Penderson. I want you to immediately stop taking those pills. I'll write you a prescription for the correct ones. I'm calling the pharmacy right now."

"Could you get the secretary to make me a copy of the prescription you wrote me a year ago for the Ortho Tri-Cyclen and make a copy of the label of the wrong prescription?"

"Of course." She nodded and headed out of the door.

While I was waiting, I calculated in my head how long I had been taking the wrong pills. It had been at least five months. The more I thought about it, the angrier I got. *This is why my behind has blown up.* It's one of the worst feelings in the world when you're not doing anything different but you're gaining weight and your clothes are getting too tight. I felt like I had an incurable disease that no one was suffering from, except me.

Before Dr. Hicks could say a formal good-bye, I waved her off and was practically running out of the office. I ran down the stairs to get to my car as soon as possible. It was just hitting ten thirty in the morning and I had the day off from work. Drug Aid was going to get a mouthful from me.

Chapter 23

"Where's the pharmacist?" I demanded after stampeding into the Drug Aid store. At least ten people were waiting in front of me. Before walking into the pharmacy, I'd turned on my tape recorder and placed it in my jacket pocket. I still had it in my purse from when I'd used it for the conference in Chicago.

"Ma'am, I'm sorry, but you'll have to wait in the back of the line just like everyone else," a pharmacy technician said.

"I'm not waiting anywhere. Unless you plan on helping me, shut up and get me someone who can. I need to speak with the head pharmacist now! I've been getting the wrong prescription for months! It wasn't even from the same doctor. How could anyone mistake the last name *Hicks* for *Penderson*? Now, as a result of this huge mistake, I've gained sixteen pounds," I hollered at the top of my lungs. I practically threw the copies I had been given at my doctor's office in her face.

"Let me see if I can help you," she replied, motioning me to another computer and picking up the papers I threw at her.

Once she put my name in the computer, I snatched the papers back. I planned on making an example out of this establishment. I was sure I wasn't the only one given the wrong prescription. Other customers may be more forgiving, but I refused to overlook this error and accept a lame apology and a discount on future prescriptions.

"Mrs. Sothers, you're right. We've been giving you the wrong prescription."

"Tell me something I don't know. Stop standing there and get me the head pharmacist."

She looked scared and had no clue what to do next.

"Katy, let me handle this," a man intervened. He began looking at the computer with her while she pointed to something.

I managed to steal a glance at the computer screen and realized the man standing in front of me was the one who'd made the mistake of filling the wrong prescription for me. His nametag matched the name on the screen.

"Ma'am, my name is Ted Bodman. I'm the head pharmacist here. It appears I was the one who mistakenly filled the wrong prescription for you. I apologize and regret you have gained sixteen pounds. However, we warn all our customers that it's their personal responsibility to make sure they're leaving the pharmacy with the correct prescription."

"It's your responsibility not to be so stupid," I shot back.

"You have made it clear to everyone in the store that you unfortunately gained sixteen pounds. As an associate of Drug Aid, I want to apologize again for the mistake. If it's any consolation, you look great. You're a very beautiful woman. Those pounds you gained probably filled the right places." He smiled, trying to boost my ego.

For a second I thought I might have heard him wrong, but when I saw the look on Katy's face, I knew I'd heard correctly. Even the women standing in line looked appalled at what he'd just said to me.

Instead of antagonizing me with compliments and telling me what I should have done, Mr. Bodman should have listened to me and shown more empathy.

I quickly grabbed three bottles of soda from a soda machine next to the computer and unscrewed the tops. Then I swung them at him. He wasted no time running for cover.

I took off one of my New Balance sneakers and jumped the counter. I found him hiding all the way in the back of the pharmacy. He was so concerned with whether or not I was going to hit him with the sneaker in my hand, he didn't even see my leg go up as I got him with a classic kick right on his dick. It felt so good. Afterward, I beat him with the shoe in my hand and kicked him repeatedly. When he tried to get up, I punched him in the face with all my might.

"You're going to jail!" he barked.

"You're going to lose your job, and the whole country is going to know what you did to me. It would be in your best interest to call your district manager and get them down here." I walked to the front of the store and reached in my pocket for my cell phone.

"Hello, Consumers on Rage," the receptionist greeted me. "This is Judy. How may I help you?"

"Hi. My name is Nya Sothers. I'm on the intersection of Virginia Beach Boulevard and Holland Road at the Drug Aid."

"Yes, I know where that is. What's going on?"

"Well, for the last five months I've been given the wrong birth control pills. It was their mistake. I went to the pharmacist to let him know what happened. He told me that the weight gain 'probably filled the right places,' if you know what I mean."

"What! This agency definitely doesn't tolerate sexual harassment of any kind."

"Then Mr. Bodman tried to shift the blame toward me, telling me that it was my responsibility to check the prescription to make sure it was correct. Checking my birth control wasn't high on the priority list. I work long hours to make ends meet." I acted like I was crying, to make damn sure I was convincing and my voice was cracking.

"So now the good old pharmacist is trying to blame you. Stay right there. I'll have a crew down there in thirty minutes," she stated and hung up the phone.

As promised, thirty minutes later the Consumers on Rage crew arrived at the drug store. We began protesting, chanting, "Sixteen pounds."

Judy and her associates were explaining what my situation to everyone who attempted to come in the store, urging them not to use Drug Aid and move their prescriptions somewhere else where their money was appreciated. Many people were outraged when they heard my story, and news was traveling fast.

Two hours later, three news channels were on the scene interviewing Judy and I. The police couldn't make us leave, and the crowd of chanters was becoming larger.

Eventually, around two hundred people, mostly women, were in the parking lot protesting. Even Tory's boss' wife, Martha, stopped by to lend her lungs to the cause. She was the loudest out of everyone.

A year earlier, Martha had undergone gastric bypass surgery. Not only was I representing myself, but also every woman who'd ever gained weight because of a wrong prescription. And the fact that weight loss and weight gain were touchy subjects helped to fuel the protest even more.

Around evening time, the president and the vice president of Drug Aid showed up. First, they spoke with Mr. Bodman then they spoke with me.

After hearing the tape recording of what Mr. Bodman had said to me, they wanted to work out a deal to get me to simply go away. They knew this situation was definitely bad for business.

Though I decided to work out a deal with them, I wasn't going to agree to anything unless I felt completely satisfied with the terms.

Mr. Bodman lost his job on the spot and decided not to press charges on me for spraying him with Sprite Zero and Coco-Cola Classic. Besides, no one would have believed that an angel like me could have given him a black eye. And the president and vice president gave each person in the crowd up to fifty dollars worth of free prescriptions.

As for me, I got a three-year paid membership to Bally's gym, which included a personal trainer and nutritionist. More importantly, I received twenty thousand dollars to simply go away, mere pennies to the Drug Aid Corporation, which could've lost millions due to bad publicity.

Only time will tell how bad a hole this protest burned in their profits. I gave a contribution of five thousand dollars to Consumers on Rage. If it wasn't for them, I may not have gotten anything until I went to court, which could have taken years. Businesses feared Consumers on Rage because of how far Judy and her associates would go to protect the almighty consumer.

Another five thousand dollars went to a local teen pregnancy shelter. Besides spending a little bit to pay for B_{12} shots, I put the rest of the money into a high-rate money market savings account. With the stock market on a losing trend, I wanted the money to be safe and secure.

Last but not least, I received my five seconds of fame, and was forever associated with the phrase "sixteen pounds." This experience taught me that corporations have zero tolerance for sexual harassment.

After getting home, taking a thirty-minute hot shower, eating chicken lo mein, and talking to Tory on the phone about the day's events, I finally had a chance to listen to all of my voice mails.

Leah thought I was uptight and needed dick on a regular basis. Plus, she wondered if she could get a free prescription of her choice.

Tara was laughing hysterically after she saw me on the news, and Yvette was proud and happy I took on the Drug Aid corporation and won.

A few days later, I went to Farm Fresh to pick up a bag of apples and a jar of Noxzema. Six ladies came up to me and chanted, "Sixteen pounds! Sixteen pounds! Sixteen pounds!" Then they smiled, cheered, and walked away.

Another lady told me I was a hero for what I did. I didn't see it that way. I was just sticking up for myself, and I planned to keep doing so in the future.

Chapter 24

"Those shoes are fierce," Leah commented to me as the four of us headed to the Aberdeen Barn for dinner. The main event tonight was the movie premiere of *Sex and the City*. To ensure we all got good seats, I splurged and paid a little extra for Director's Hall tickets online. Director's Hall allows you to reserve your own seats from a virtual map online. Although we didn't have to worry about rushing to get good seats, we still wanted to arrive at the AMC Lynnhaven theatre at least a half an hour before the show started. Even though gas prices were rising every week, I knew women would scrounge up the money to come out with their friends and probably even drag their boyfriends and husbands to see this movie.

"Thanks," I replied, remembering how much I paid for my pair of black signature Manolo Blahnik shoes.

All of us decided to put on our best dresses in honor of the fabulous Carrie Bradshaw. We planned on enjoying the night to the fullest.

"I'm stuffed," Leah said, after taking the last bite of her Maryland crab cake.

"I'm full too," I told her, "but I'll manage to get in a few bites of popcorn and sip on a cherry ice soda."

Just then, someone's cell phone rang.

"Oh, it's Rob!" Tara exclaimed. "I haven't heard from my baby all day." She left the table and walked toward the bathroom.

"I ate way too much. Now I'll have to suck in my gut. It's going to be hard with this dress." Leah took a deep breath.

Tara sat back down at the table. "Stephanie has pulled yet another stunt. Rob has had it. He's finished with her."

"She is the mother of their son," Yvette responded. "He can't be done with her. He'll be dealing with her for the rest of his life."

"What happened?" I asked.

"Well, Stephanie flew in from Atlanta to drop Ryan off. Once she got here, she wanted Rob to pay for a hotel room for her."

"Of course, he said no," Yvette declared.

"Damn right! He wouldn't dare do it. So she copped an attitude because she had to pay for a hotel room and a rental car. She figured Rob would be toting her around, but that didn't happen either. This afternoon, she went to his job.

He was in a meeting trying to persuade several doctors on a new blood pressure medication. It's taken three years for this drug to even get approved. She stormed in the room ranting about how Ryan doesn't have any food to eat or clothes to wear, embarrassing Rob in front of his colleagues. To top it off, she had the poor kid in nothing but a pull-up soaked in doo-doo and a snotty nose. Finally, security got a hold of her and escorted her out."

"Does Rob have Ryan now?" Yvette asked.

"Yeah. He took him home to bathe, feed, and clothe him. We always keep extra sets of clothes and shoes for him at the house. He had Ryan up until an hour ago. Rob met Stephanie at the nearest police station, so she could take Ryan back. He figured it was the best place to meet, just in case she tried something else."

"Did he get fired? How did his coworkers react?" Leah asked.

"No. From what I hear, his boss has baby mama drama too, so he understood the situation. Stephanie is crazy though. Rob has been giving her four hundred and ninety-five dollars a month since Ryan was born. He's never missed a month, and they've never gone to court for custody or child support or anything like that. Then she calls him one night and tells him she needs more money than what he's giving her. When Rob told her four hundred and ninety-five dollars was more than enough, she flipped out, threatening to take him to court for it. Now, he's refusing to give her any more child support until they go before a judge. I've never heard him so angry on the phone."

I nodded. "It does need to be court-ordered."

"Ryan needs to be potty-trained," Leah said. "Isn't he five years old now?"

"Yes, it's ridiculous. Stephanie feels it's okay with her if he pees and poops in the bed at night. She doesn't press the issue. When I met Rob, Ryan was only a few months old. Through the years, Stephanie's been mad and bitter, refusing to accept that Rob doesn't want her anymore. Hell, he married me, and she still doesn't get the hint. Now, she does things just to get a reaction out of him. Stephanie doesn't bother to look my way because she knows I'm not putting up with any of her crap. It only took one time to put that wench in her place. Three years ago, she sneaked upstairs, claiming she had to change the baby. Instead, she cut up a bunch of my panties and thongs. Since then, she's no longer allowed in my house. I told Rob back then, if he wanted us to stay together, I didn't want to hear about that day-to-day bullshit Stephanie was putting him through."

I giggled. "I remember that episode."

"Rob should still pay her child support," Yvette added.

"I told him the same thing. Ryan still needs his diapers and clothes and all that. He went down to the courthouse to try to get an earlier date, so we don't have to wait so long. He also filed for full custody, which I hope comes out in his favor. I wouldn't mind having Ryan around for good."

"You mean Rob and you having Ryan all the time?" I asked.

"Yes." Tara nodded, smiling.

"Says the late-night party girl," Leah added.

"To be honest, I love Rob and Ryan. He's a good kid. All the little boy needs is some stability, structure, and love. When Ryan stays at our house, he's potty-trained. I guess what I'm trying to say is, I'm willing to give up going out almost every weekend for the greater good of my marriage and family."

"Did you tell Rob the same thing?" I asked.

"Yes, I sure did. I'm getting older. Going out is fun, and I will probably still hang out, just not as much as I do now. My priorities are changing. But don't worry, Leah, I'll always be your true party buddy at heart." Tara winked at Leah.

"You're growing up," Yvette told her, and we all started laughing.

Chapter 25

I stepped onto the third floor of the hospital carrying a small plastic bag in my hand containing a cranberry and apple muffin.

"Thank God, you're here," Donna blurted out.

"What's going on?" I asked, stopping in my tracks.

"Girl, Smokey was throwing up practically the entire night. He's known for eating dirt, so I figured his upset stomach would subside. My husband took him to the vet this morning. Based on the X-ray, he ate a sock."

"What!"

"That's right. A sock. It's going to cost twenty-three hundred dollars to repair his intestines. We just put a new roof on the house. I don't know what we're going to do. The kids would be devastated if we have to put him down."

"Yeah, the kids would be heartbroken," I added, shaking my head.

"Can you cover my patients? I need to go home and sort this out." Donna rubbed her temples.

"Yes, I sure will."

"Thank you so much. Right now, I only have one patient. Her name is Paula Caplin. Two days ago, she had a miscarriage. Based on her chart, this has been the third miscarriage from invitro fertilization. She's been crying and is very feisty. I put in for a psych consult; the doctor is in with her now."

"As long as she doesn't throw things at me like Mrs. Bulford attempted to do last week, I can deal with her mouth."

Fifteen hours later, tired and ready to go home, I was coming out of the main entrance hospital doors when I found Tara standing by my car.

"Hey," I greeted her.

She took a deep breath. "I'm pregnant."

I guess she didn't want to waste any time getting to the point. "Congratulations! It's the best news I've heard all month."

"Thanks." She gave me a hug.

"Why the long face?"

"It hasn't sunk in yet that I'm going to be a mother. Rob and I will be responsible for another human being for the rest of our lives. He's so excited. Both of our parents are ecstatic about the news. For a while now, Dad has been putting a bug in my ear about wanting to be a grandfather. I just can't believe I'm going to have a baby." Tara giggled.

"I can't believe it either. When are you due?"

"I'm due in May. Right now, my head is spinning."

"How about you come to my house for a little bit? I have leftover pork chops sitting in the fridge. I'll make you my famous antipasto platter to go with it, and we'll call the girls so we can all eat dinner together."

"Well, I never said I wasn't hungry. Plus, I love that antipasto platter with the garlic-infused olives. They're so yummy.

"I'll follow you home," she said, rubbing her hands together.

"Great. I just need to stop by the store and pick up some dessert."

Last night, I'd made stuffed pork chops with sautéed spinach and bread crumbs, along with fresh steamed artichoke hearts smothered in parmesan reggiano cheese and brown rice. All I needed to do was make the antipasto platter, and tonight's dinner was done. For dessert, I planned on picking up pineapple cupcakes with cream cheese icing with colorful flowers made out of sugar and food coloring on top. I just hoped the girls didn't have any plans for tonight and would be able to join Tara and I for dinner on such short notice.

"Hi," Yvette greeted us when we opened the front door.

"Hey," we replied in unison.

"Glad my day is over. I'm starving. Feed me." Leah charged into the house. I hadn't seen her standing behind Yvette.

"Hello to you too, Leah," I said, rolling my eyes. "The food is in the oven. The platter is on the kitchen table. It's funny how you never find the time to cook us dinner at your house."

Leah shrugged her shoulders. "That's what I have Nelson for."

"I'm pregnant. I'm due in May. This bad girl is terrified," Tara blurted out after popping a piece of salami and an olive in her mouth.

"Bad girls can be great mothers too," I expressed, trying to ease her mind.

"Aaah, you're joining the club. It's about time someone else out of the group have a little one. Now, Michael and Natalie will have someone to play with. Those two will love the baby as if it was their own brother or sister. I can't wait to share the good news with them." Yvette gave Tara a high-five and hugged her.

Leah giggled. "Better you than me. No more apple martinis for you." Then she gave Tara a hug.

"That's right," I said.

"Let's eat and talk," Leah demanded, running into the kitchen.

After eating, we watched *Crooklyn*, a movie we hadn't seen in years. Without a doubt, everybody's favorite scene was when the aunt pulled the couch out, only to discover the dog they had been searching for all day.

Chapter 26

Today, it cost almost fifty dollars to fill up my tank. The gas station down the street was no longer offering full service. They wanted to make sure customers paid the cashier before pumping to ward off people who would pull up, and then drive off when their tank was filled.

Not in the mood to cook, I went into the store looking for a DiGiorno pizza with cheese only and a pre-made salad.

When I got home, I ate my store-bought dinner and headed to my bedroom to go to sleep. I wasn't looking forward to the twelve-hour shift I had the next day.

Just as I felt I was falling into a deep sleep, I felt a subtle kiss on my forehead and then on my cheek. Then my thighs being caressed gently by masculine hands. I felt my pussy getting moist with every caress.

Am I having a wet dream?

Then the hands began to explore my body even more.

I could hear a song by Stevie Wonder playing in the background. *What was the name of that song again? Yes, now I remember.* "Send One Your Love."

Just then, a warm body settled next to me in the bed.

Mmmm, this is turning out to be a great dream. Come to Mama, I thought, spreading my legs apart.

"Baby, I missed you so much. I want you," I heard a man's voice whisper.

Wait a minute. That sounded real. Maybe I'm not dreaming. I opened my eyes just in time to see Tory reach over to pull the lace ribbon tied on my nightgown.

"Tory, what are you doing here?" I shrieked.

"Shhh," he said, slipping off my nightgown and black panties.

We began to kiss. I didn't want to let his tongue go. I missed him so much.

"Baby, I left the rehab center. It was time for me to come home to you. I almost forgot the code on the security system." He lifted me off the bed.

We couldn't keep our hands off each other. If Tory didn't already have his clothes off, I would have ripped them off of him.

"What did Dr. Waters say about—?"

"No questions. We'll talk in the morning. Right now, you know what I want and need."

He let my hair down and pushed me up against the wall. He managed to kiss his way down to my pussy. He lifted me up with my legs on his shoulders and began to flick his tongue against my clit over and over again.

What a ride! I thought

"On the way here, all I could think about was the first time we did it. I love to taste your pussy. Cum on my tongue, baby."

"Aaah, if you insist," I cooed while cumming. My body shook uncontrollably.

Our eyes locked.

"I love you," Tory whispered.

"I love you so much," I managed to get out in between breaths.

Tory let me slide back down to the carpet and laid me on my back. As his tongue licked my nipples, his finger played with my clit. I didn't want this endless pleasure to stop.

I slightly arched my back as I felt him slide his python inside my soaking pussy. Slow, deep, long strokes followed as we kissed again.

After he came, I rolled the chair from the office room into our bedroom and ordered him to sit down in it. As he sat in the chair, his head rolled back while I deep-throated him. I couldn't help but to climb on his dick and tighten my pussy muscles around it again.

"Nya, that feels good. You know I like it tight."

Sweat was dripping from both of our foreheads. We didn't care.

Tory picked me up, threw me on the bed, and turned me around to enter me from the back.

"I missed this dick."

"He's back for good now," he declared, pulling my hair and giving me deep, hard strokes.

This time, we both came together and collapsed on the bed.

Chapter 27

The next morning, desperately wanting to find out why Tory was home so early, I tiptoed downstairs to use my cell phone. Dr. Waters hadn't given me a definitive date of his return home, so I didn't know if Tory was scheduled to come home at all. Yes, I loved the idea of having him home with me again, but I was ready for him to stay away from me for as long as it took to get all the necessary treatments, rather than spend a lifetime with him as a drunk.

Once in the living room, I noticed a black bag under the chair. Enclosed was an empty bottle of Bacardi rum, two bottles of Absolut vodka, and a bottle of Chivas Regal scotch. He didn't make a good attempt at hiding it from me. I thought, on our last visit, he was making progress.

I ran in the kitchen. I needed answers right away. I ransacked the drawer, looking for Dr. Water's cell phone number.

"Dr. Waters speaking," he answered the phone.

"Hi, Dr. Waters. This is Nya, Tory Sothers' wife."

"Nya, you're just the person I need to talk to. Yesterday evening, I left you a voice mail on your cell phone and home phone about the status of your husband."

Last night, too tired, I didn't bother answering either one of my phones. "What's going on? Why was Tory released so early?" I inquired, not beating around the bush. I didn't want Tory to wake up and overhear my conversation.

"Last week, Tory and the other patients at the treatment center went on a retreat in the woods. It's good for them to get out. Most of the patients embrace the opportunity. At first, Tory was enjoying himself. Then, after a while, he demanded to go back to the center. I decided to go back with him. We had a talk and—"

"Why did he leave?"

Tears began to stream down my face. I would be very disappointed if Tory had left against orders. That would prove to me that he didn't seem to realize that his actions affected other people's lives. Especially me, his wife. His mom was also hoping that he would complete the program, no matter how long it took. It would break her heart if she found out he dropped out early.

"Mrs. Sothers, it boils down to this. Within the walls of the treatment center, Tory can handle coping with the loss of his father and getting a grip on the alcoholism. In his words, and I quote, 'Doc, this place is a protective shield for me.' Once he's outside in the real world, he simply can't handle it. Last night, he hopped on a plane and left. Plus, I think he missed you as well. Right now, Tory doesn't realize he can make it through this. Until he makes that decision, it's going to be a vicious cycle of him relapsing over and over again."

"I can't believe he left. He damn sure fooled his family and me. So has he been kicked out of the program?" I asked between sobs.

"No, no, no. He's welcome to come back. If this program doesn't work, I can recommend others. Nya—excuse me, pardon my manners. May I call you Nya?"

"Yes."

"The most difficult battle is the one within yourself. This may be a long hard road for Tory. I hope I'm not crossing any boundaries with what I am about to say, Nya. You may need to make the decision of whether to stick around or not. Each person has a limit to what she or he can bear. I know it hurts to realize a bottle is more important than you. Please try to remember, alcoholism is a disease. Please don't hesitate to call me if you have any other questions, or if Tory wants to come back."

"Dr. Waters, thank you for taking the time to speak with me. Hopefully, I can get him back into the program," I said, disappointment and resentment in my voice.

After pressing the end button on my cell phone, I dialed Steven. He couldn't believe his brother had walked out like that. We both decided that perhaps he could talk some sense into him.

I threw my cell phone on the kitchen counter and ran upstairs to our bedroom.

Tory smiled after I walked through the bedroom door. He placed the empty bottle on the nightstand. "Chivas Regal scotch was my father's favorite drink."

"Hmm, I don't remember your father drinking himself to death. Did you know your father's favorite thing to do was teach? Follow in his footsteps that way."

"I know you're pissed. I overheard you talking to Dr. Waters. It never fails. You almost always seem to get up before me. I married an early bird. I tried to go downstairs and hide that bag in another place, but of course, you beat me to it. Right now, I got a huge headache and don't feel like hearing your damn mouth, or feel your wrath about my drinking. I just came home.

You should be fixing me something to eat. Grits, eggs, biscuits, and a glass of orange juice would be nice. Thank you," he said, a smirk on his face.

"Starve, for all I care." I folded my arms.

"I missed you. I put last night on my top-five-most-memorable-times-of-having-sex-with-you list." He inched closer to me.

"Don't even think about touching me!" I yelled, looking into his eyes. "Why did you leave?"

"Please, don't yell. I can't stand it when you yell. Your voice pierces through my ears." He shook his head, moving away from me.

"Are you going to tell me or not? You owe your family and me an explanation. I'm so glad we don't have kids together. You don't give a fuck about anybody but yourself. Did you know how many days and nights your mother has worried herself over you?"

"My father is dead; yours is not. Can't you understand that?"

"Using your father's death as a reason to drink yourself to death is not an excuse."

"I don't think I'm strong enough to cope outside in the real world. I just can't. Are you happy now?" He barked. "You got your answer."

"Go back to the program. Dr. Waters is willing to take you back. Or you can try another program. Tory, I thought I made myself clear the first time. It's either the bottle or me."

"Nya, don't do this."

"Don't do what? I'm trying to save your life. Alcoholism can kill you. Alcohol ruins your liver, and they're hard to come by. Any organ donation program would hesitate to give an alcoholic a healthy liver over someone who doesn't drink. You have to learn to cope with life. You have a lot of thinking to do. I'm not the most perfect woman in the world, but I go above and beyond to take care of you and keep you happy. You, me, and our possible future kids can have a good life together. Taking vacations, breakfast in bed, oversleeping, and growing old together is what we dreamed of. Please don't throw it away. I called your brother, Steven. He and Anne waiting for you at his house. They want to talk to you."

"I can't believe you told them I was here. I'm not ready to face them or my mom." Tory walked out of the room and headed down the stairs.

I chased after him, screaming at the top of my lungs, "We're trying to save your life! Why is that concept not getting through your damn brain?"

He was too fast for me. Before I knew it, he grabbed his truck keys from the table in the foyer and slammed the door behind him.

Too tired and stressed to go to work, I called Jill to let her know I wouldn't be coming in. My stomach was killing me.

I quickly ran upstairs and searched through my medicine cabinet to pop a pill in my mouth for the ulcer, which was pulsating in my stomach. Now, I regretted not telling Tory about the ulcer. If he knew, it would have made him feel guilty.

While in the shower, I cried. I was hoping Tory would pick me over a bottle of alcohol and we could spend the rest of our lives together.

A few hours later, pacing my bedroom wasn't helping at all, so I went to lie down. I had ignored the house phone and my cell phone all day. I didn't want to talk to anyone right now.

The biggest fear wearing on my mind was not knowing what his decision would be. I wasn't prepared to accept him choosing alcohol over me, but I had no other option but to accept it and deal with it if he did.

Before I knew it, I drifted off to sleep in my robe.

Chapter 28

When I woke up, there was a yellow rose lying next to me with a card. Enclosed was a letter.

> *Dear Nya,*
> *I have been telling you over and over again that my father is DEAD. Mom, Steven, Anne and you all act as if you want to go on with your lives. I can't face the truth he's never coming back again. Without the alcohol, I can't cope. I'm sorry.*
> *Love always,*
> *Tory*

Where the hell did he go? I thought, looking for my cell phone.

Once downstairs, I quickly dialed his cell phone number. It was disconnected. I called Verizon Wireless, only to find out he had disconnected the phone without a forwarding number.

His truck was parked in the driveway and the truck keys and wallet were on the kitchen counter.

I had seven missed calls on my cell phone, all from Steven and Anne. Instead of dialing either one of their numbers, I threw some clothes on and raced over to Steven's house. I got dressed so fast, I accidentally tore a hole in my favorite grape-colored velour pants. At that point, I didn't even care. Tory was far more important.

"Did you talk to him? Where is he?" I asked Steven after he opened his front door and I barged in.

"Nya, Tory is gone. He came here to tell us to stop wasting our breath about him giving up alcohol. He ignored everything we had to say to him. Nothing we said or did can convince him to seek help again. We talked to him for over an hour. My brother is a grown man, and none of us can force him to do anything."

"He left me a note." I showed it to him.

He read it, and so did Anne.

"Nya, Tory has made his decision. There's nothing we can do about it," Anne whimpered, hugging me.

I couldn't feel my legs. It was almost as if I was in shock. I couldn't believe he just left me. *How could he do this to his family and me?* "I'm going to the police station."

"Why?" Steven questioned.

"To fill out a missing person's report."

"Let me drive you. Nya, you're in no condition to drive anywhere."

It seemed like it took forever before we got to the police station. Each second I realized Tory was gone felt more like hours.

"I need to fill out a missing person's report please," I explained to the police officer after walking up to the counter.

Anne took me over to the waiting area to sit down, and Steven began explaining the situation to the police officer.

The next thing I know, the police officer came walking over to me. "Mrs. Sothers, I'm Officer Ross, your brother-in-law explained what happened to your husband. Unfortunately, under these circumstances, we're unable to fill out a missing person's report because, technically, he's not missing. He chose to leave you. He not only told you, but his brother and sister as well. In addition, we cannot file a report until he has been missing for more than twenty-four hours."

"Don't say he left me!" I snapped.

"Ma'am, I know this must be difficult for you."

"Please . . . can you bend the rules?" I begged. "It would make me feel better if the report was taken seriously. He's probably drunk somewhere and may get hurt. At least, the missing report may help to locate him sooner."

"Mrs. Sothers, I'm sorry, but I can not make any exceptions to our rules and policies."

I didn't want to accept his response, so I refused to leave, demanding that even more officers listen to my story and try to find Tory.

After a while of my ranting, Anne called Yvette, Tara, and Leah. She must have retrieved their numbers from my cell phone. Even with them there, I still refused to leave.

The officers advised Steven that I had to calm down or leave the premises, or they would have me arrested me for disorderly conduct. Steven had no choice but to take me out of the police station kicking and screaming.

I couldn't bear going back to my house, so Yvette and Leah took me to my parents' house.

I stayed in my old room over the next several weeks and didn't do much of anything. I didn't go to work. I couldn't go to work. The only person I called was Jill. I gave her a vague explanation of what happened and requested time off. She was very understanding and told me take all the time I needed.

The whole situation felt surreal. It felt like I was never going to feel better. My fucking husband left me for an alcohol bottle.

I was driving myself crazy every morning by checking our bank accounts and credit card accounts online to see if there was any recent activity from Tory's card.

I was hoping to locate Tory myself. I even hired a private investigator, which turned up nothing. Tory had vanished and didn't want to be found. *Was coming back here too hard to bear?*

Every night, I prayed God would bring Tory back to me. At this point I didn't know if he was alive, but it felt as if the person I married had died. Days and nights seemed to clump together.

Yvette, Leah, Tara, and Mommy tried their best to be there for me, but I shut them out and didn't want to be bothered. All I wanted to do was think about my husband, and if I did talk to any of them, it would be about him. They were probably sick of it by now. Mom even brought the pastor of her church to pray for me.

My cell phone was with me at all times. I wished Tory would call me so I could hear his voice. Until now, I didn't realize how much I truly loved him. Was this all a bad dream? Did I deserve such cruelty to my heart?

Chapter 29

It was an unusually warm day for winter. The temperature crept up into the mid-sixties. I woke up feeling helpless and hopeless. I was too drained to cry another tear. I didn't want to move, I didn't want to go on with my life. All I wanted to do was stare at the wall in my old bedroom, have my cell phone right by my side, and reminisce about the most cherished times with my husband. I didn't want anyone feeling sorry for me.

Surprisingly, out of everyone, Leah, my self-centered sister, came around most often to check on me. She didn't even insult me like she normally would.

My cell phone and house phone mailboxes were full. Unless the messages were from Tory, I didn't care to listen to them. Even if Jill fired me for being out so long, I didn't care. Being an experienced registered nurse, I could get a job at any hospital or medical facility.

There was a knock at the door.

"Come in," I announced.

"Morning, sunshine." Daddy greeted me with a smile.

"Hey, Daddy," I responded, not smiling.

"Nya, one of the qualities you got from me is not beating around the bush. I'm your father, and I hate to see you like this. So many nights I've came to check on you at least three times before I lay my head down, and you look a mess."

"My husband left me," I whimpered.

"I know your husband left you. We all know your husband left you. It's sad and unfortunate. Right now, I'm not Tory's biggest fan. While he's been out drinking and God knows what else, I've been cutting the grass at your house and emptying out your mailbox every day so the mailman won't send back your mail."

"Did Tory send me a letter?"

"No," he replied, shaking his head.

"It's not his style to write letters, anyway, and mail them. Leaving a letter on my pillow is more like him."

"This isn't about Tory. I'm in here for you. Look, Nya, I know you're devastated he left you. All I'm asking you to do is, don't let Tory's shortcomings define your life. You've done all the crying you can and have had the biggest pity party for yourself. Now, it's not going to be easy to cope without him, but you got to try to enjoy yourself again. I haven't seen you smile in weeks. Your momma has been so worried about you."

"The last thing I want is for Mommy and you to be worried about me."

"Well, give us a reason to put our minds at ease."

"Daddy, I think you're right. I do need to get up and pull myself together."

"Now, that's my daughter talking. Put some clothes on, I want to take you to lunch."

"All right." The idea of food had enticed me for the first time in a while.

"I have two surprises for you," Daddy announced, heading outside of my bedroom door.

"What is it?"

"First, I got your momma to sew up those grape-colored velour pants that you love wearing. She noticed they had a hole in them. I would have bought you a new set, but knowing you, this is better."

"You got that right." I was happy my pants were back intact.

"For your second surprise, I bought two pounds of those sweet Rainier cherries. I know they have distinctive colors and are hard to come by around this time," he said with a look of accomplishment.

"Daddy, they're not in season. How did you get them so early?" I said already starting to eat a few.

"I got a buddy down at the Farmers Market on Princess Anne Road. While you freshen up and put some clothes on, I'll go put the rest in the refrigerator." He headed out of my bedroom door.

"Daddy?"

"Yeah, baby?"

"Thanks for everything. I guess I owe you guys some rent for as long as I've been staying here," I said, smiling again.

"You're welcome. Nonsense. I'm not taking half of a penny from you. Now, hurry up. It's almost one o'clock, and you know I got to eat before I take my medication. A cheeseburger and onion rings dipped in ketchup are calling my name at Fuddruckers. Don't tell your momma. She'll be on me about my cholesterol and blood pressure." He winked at me.

I giggled. "I promise I won't tell her. Give me fifteen minutes, and I'll be right downstairs."

"Sure, baby." He hugged me.

Later on that week, when I finally returned home, I put my wedding ring in the drawer and swore to never look at it again.

Chapter 30

Besides a few overdraft fees being accumulated due to transfers not being completed on time, Rome did pretty well without me monitoring the accounts for the restaurant. Fortunately, I had the bank refund over a hundred dollars worth of fees back to the business checking account. BankFIRST, fully aware that mistakes happen, recommended we get a line of credit to link to the account, just in case it happened again. Thanks to great advertising and loyal customers, the restaurant was doing very well. And based on deposits, bills, and payroll, from a business perspective, we were still staying above water.

"Hey, Nya, how are you doing?" Rome asked before giving me a hug.

"Back from the dead, I guess," I responded, shrugging my shoulders. He and I had agreed to meet at the restaurant to talk before the doors opened for business.

"Here's your favorite, a virgin raspberry daiquiri with two maraschino cherries and a slice of orange," he announced after placing it at the bar.

"Thanks." I nodded my head.

"If you don't mind me asking, have you talked to Tory?" he inquired after taking a deep breath. Rome had an expression on his face as if he was expecting me to take a pan and hit him with it just for asking about the now infamous Tory.

"No," I quickly commented after taking a few sips of my daiquiri.

Anyone could tell by my body language that I didn't want to talk about Tory or his whereabouts. Tory had made his own choice to leave a life he once cherished. His boss Irv still had high hopes that he'd come back and kept him on the payroll. Through the years Tory worked for Irv, he'd made millions for him. The fact that the two of them were so close was another reason why Tory's check was still being deposited directly into our joint checking account. At least Tory was still paying for the mortgage.

Pain, hurt and uncertainty lay in my heart. I hadn't begun the healing process. To be honest, I was still in shock that he left. Right now, the only two men in my life were God and Daddy.

"Thanks for coming down here to see me," Rome said.

"Sure, no problem. Listen, first I would like to apologize for my absence here at the restaurant. I want you to know—"

"Nya, I completely understand how devastated you were and probably still are."

"Well, I'm back now with fresh ideas. Despite Tory's choice to leave, I still want to remain business partners with you. Besides, I consider you a friend."

We shook hands.

"Let's hear those ideas you mentioned." He nodded.

"I wanted to suggest an all-you-can-eat buffet on Tuesday or Wednesday nights. It can spice up the week for people's taste buds because it won't be limited to just one type of dish. Also, on Mondays through Thursdays between the hours of four and six p.m., we can have drink specials and offer half off appetizers. And perhaps you can create daily lunch specials. Basically, my goal is to attract more customers and offer more affordable prices. A lot of businesses are closing down, and the unemployment line is increasing. I want the community to feel like this a good family-friendly neighborhood restaurant with reasonable prices. I want to make sure business stays good. We couldn't ask for a better team here, and I would hate to have to lay off any staff.

They have families to take care of too. So what do
you think?"

"I don't want to lay anyone off either. Plus,
the staff has been on their A-game because of
the fear of getting the boot due to the economy.
Your ideas are catchy and well thought out. I
think we should continue to have a featured dish
every night. Also, on the weekends, we should
introduce a dinner special at two for twenty-five
dollars. It will include an appetizer, two entrees,
and a dessert."

"Your suggestions are a go-ahead in my book.
I also want to start doing radio advertising. I
know a sales representative who can give us a
great deal on radio airtime on 103 JAMZ, 95.7,
92.9, 101.3, and 105.3. I don't want to spend no
more than two thousand."

"Sounds good to me. Can you stay for lunch?"

"Not really. My boss asked me to come in an
hour early today. She wants to discuss something with me. I'll tell you what—can you whip
a to-go box full of entrées to feed about six to
seven people? I'm sure my coworkers would
appreciate it.

"Let me grab an apron."

Food always put smiles on people's faces especially when you work twelve- to sixteen-hour
shifts. Also, it was my way of saying thank you to
all the coworkers who called to check up on me.

A few weeks ago, I'd returned to work and was welcomed back with open arms from everyone. It felt good to be back on my normal routine. Jill confided in me that her own father was an alcoholic and was suffering from cirrhosis of the liver. You never know what other people are going through in their own lives.

Chapter 31

"I smell food," David blurted out as he headed toward me.

Karen and Evita followed close behind him.

"Back away, you're not on my favorites list," I said to him jokingly.

"Come on, Nya, I've been working a twelve-hour shift. Coffee and stale peanuts aren't hitting the spot. At home, the only thing in my pantry is beef-flavored Oodles of Noodles."

"I'm starving." Evita took the bags from my hands.

"Who said any of this was for you guys?" I asked, a grin on my face.

"We'll take this to the nurses' lounge. We'll give David, our hospital crumb-snatcher, a little bit." Karen told me, "Jill is asking for you."

"Where is she?"

"In her office."

"Don't worry, we'll save some for you," Evita said.

"I'm not hungry. Eat all you want. I bought it for the staff on shift."

"Hmm! This food will be gone by the end of the hour," I heard Karen say as I approached Jill's office.

I knocked on the half-open door and made my way in. "Jill, you wanted to see me."

A woman who looked familiar was sitting across from her.

"Nya, yes," she greeted me with a smile. "Please come in and have a seat."

"Hi," I said to the woman and sat down in the chair next to her.

"This is Carla Flax. You delivered her son about two years ago."

"We meet again. I thought you looked familiar. What I remember most is your daughter Rose that came to visit you. She was around seven and a real cutie pie." I smiled. Rose took a real liking to me and followed me everywhere she could during the time her mother and little brother were in the hospital. I didn't mind at all. She was so pleasant and full of life.

"That's why I'm here. You see, Nya, Rose has been diagnosed with a rare heart disease. Fortunately, with hopes and prayers from our family, friends, and church, she was able to get a heart transplant. However, her body didn't adjust to the new heart. There's nothing more we can do, and she doesn't have that long to live."

"I'm so sorry," I whimpered, placing my right hand on my chest. The mere thought of a child of mine dying was something I couldn't even imagine.

"Thank you. I was able to enroll her in the Make-A-Wish Foundation. One of the things she would to like to do is meet The Cheetah Girls. She'd also like to shadow you for a day as a nurse. Ever since Rose met you two years ago, you're all she talks about and says she wanted to become a nurse just like you. So all I'm asking is if she can come to work with you for a day," Carla proposed to me in tears.

"Of course, she can. I will make it fun for her. Whatever day is convenient for you, please let me know. I will make myself available."

"Tuesdays seems to be better days for her, and she's less tired. If it's all right with you, I will be here next Tuesday with her. Thank you so much. She's going to be so excited." Carla stood to give me a hug.

"You're welcome."

Until today, I didn't know how much of an impact I made on people.

Later that night, I went to a medical store and made a rush delivery of custom-made medical scrubs in The Cheetah Girls print in Rose's size. The hospital donated a basket filled with the latest DVD from The Cheetah Girls, an iTunes gift card to download their music, teddy bears, stickers, journals, a stethoscope, blood pressure cuffs, kid-friendly medical DVDs, and a nametag especially designed for her.

Chapter 32

I had my good days and bad days. Some mornings, after waking up, I would even wonder what kind of day I would have. The good ones had laughter and me enjoying the simple things of life and feeling on top of my game. The bad ones were filled with me having a horrible attitude, feeling depressed, pissed off, and not wanting to be bothered with anyone. Those days consisted of me eating whatever I thought could help me feel better, especially fried fish and French fries cooked hovered in a thick batter. One thing I always had on good or bad days was a to-hell-with-them mentality toward men.

Today, it didn't help much that Chris Caliente on 103 JAMZ had her show, *Girl Talk* featuring a lady about three years older than me going through almost the same thing as me. Her husband had been in and out of her life, hooked on heroin. She was confused about whether to stay with him or not. What kept her with him for nine

years was their three children. One caller advised
her to be patient, to pray and urge him to go to
rehab.

After I heard that, the tension around my head
tightened. *Why does she or I have to be patient?
Men thinking and feeling they can come and go
as they please is bullshit. Tory left me for some
goddamn alcohol and wasn't looking back. He
had a wife and a home to take care of, but it
wasn't important enough to him.*

I couldn't grab my cordless phone from the
table fast enough to dial the number to the radio
station.

"Hi, this is Chris Caliente, you're on *Girl
Talk*," she announced.

I was truly satisfied to get through the line on
the second try. "Hey, Chris, this is Nya, I just
wanted to start off saying that I love your show."

"Nya, thank you very much. So what's your
thought about the topic of the day?"

"Well, I don't agree with the last caller. A few
months ago, I gave my husband an ultimatum.
It was either me or the drinking. He had at least
a day to think about it. Ultimately, he chose the
booze. Me, personally, I refuse to be a yo-yo for
a man. My husband is a selfish bastard and did
nothing but take me for granted. I deserve better,
and so does that woman. The lady who wrote the

show should follow in my footsteps and move on with her life. Yeah, it's hard, but I take it moment by moment and get through with the help of my friends and family. When she wants to take him back, think about the unforgettable memories he's missed with his kids, and when those bills pile up every month and he's nowhere in sight to contribute." I took a deep breath.

Two weeks ago, I had changed the locks and four-digit pin code to the security system. I refused to let Tory think our house had a revolving front door for him to come and go as he pleased. I didn't know if he would ever come back at this point, but if he ever tried, it definitely wasn't going to be easy for him.

"Nya, thanks for sharing."

Since I hadn't been to the gym in weeks, I decided to go first thing in the morning. My alarm went off promptly at six, and I was at the gym by six thirty. Yeah, I was definitely an early riser. The next day, while looking into the mirror, I realized those last extra pounds I'd gained had finally melted off me. Stress will do it every time.

My trainer Joe worked with me for an hour. While using the punching bag for thirty minutes, I imagined Tory's face on it. It helped blow off some steam. To be honest, I was still deeply hurt and angry that he had thrown away our dreams together like some old-ass leftovers.

My bad attitude toward men continued to linger in the air. Any man who got in my way was going to feel my wrath.

The next thing on my agenda was to head home for a hot shower and breakfast. Granola and ripe blueberries mixed with vanilla yogurt got my energy going.

My day was off to such a great start. I didn't want to go to work. It didn't help to know that the central air system had broken down at the hospital. Severely injured patients and intensive care unit patients were being taken to other nearby hospitals that had the luxury of a working system. To make matters worse, a massive heat wave in the city had been going on for six days.

Before getting on the elevator to head to the second floor, I closed my eyes, hoping to make it through the day. I had eleven hours and fifty minutes left to go on my twelve-hour shift. Just then, my cell phone vibrated. It was a text message from Tara.

Yesterday, I heard you on the radio. If you still need to vent, I'm here for you. Love you much.

"What floor?" I asked a man that got on the elevator with me. He was dressed in a work suit, and his mouth covered with a white mask.

"Second floor please."

I noticed on his front left side shoulder a logo that read *Air Professionals*.

"Okay," I said, pressing 2. I had to press it three times to light up. *That's strange*, I thought to myself.

"How are you doing today?" he asked, trying to make conversation.

Lucky for me, this ride would be over shortly.

"It would be better if the central air unit was working properly. Patients and their family members are screaming in our faces about it."

"Well, we tried to fix it by cleaning it out."

"It didn't work."

"My team and I are aware of it. Now, we just received word the higher-ups in this hospital approved for a brand-new unit to be installed. It won't be here until tomorrow."

"Good. I'll let my coworkers know. The hospital administration isn't telling us anything."

"I'm glad I could give you the exclusive scoop. The old unit is about twenty-four years old. I'm surprised it lasted this long."

"It broke down at the worst time."

The elevator suddenly stopped, so I started to press 2.

"Things happen that way. Be patient. Everything always happens for a reason. Good or bad, they happen at the time they are meant to happen." He nodded.

I continued to press the button, but the elevator wasn't moving, and the button wasn't lighting up.

The last thing I needed was a stranger schooling me on how and why things happen. I would have told him to spare me his philosophical thoughts, but right now, I just wanted to be out of this hot elevator.

"Have you been here long?"

"For the most part, I've been here since eight o'clock this morning."

"Have you heard of any problems going on with the elevators?"

"No, not that I'm aware of."

After I pressed the red emergency button, a voice came on over the intercom.

"Hi, folks, this is the hospital administrator, Fred Sachs, we have called the fire department and they will be arriving shortly. Six out of the ten elevators have stopped midway. Please try to remain calm. We will get you out as soon as we can. Thank you for your patience, and I am sorry for the inconvenience."

"Damn it! I have patients to take care of." I dialed the nurses' station on the second floor.

"You can't do anything about it, Nya," the man announced after reading my nametag.

The phone line was busy, so I dialed Donna's cell phone number.

"Nya?"

I was surprised I had reception in the elevator. "Yeah, it's me. I'm stuck in the elevator. Can you take care of my patients till they pry me out of here?"

"Of course, I will. Are you all right?" How many people are with you?"

"I'm fine and grateful to have a couple of frosted blueberry Pop-Tarts and a few bottles of green tea to help me get by. It's just me and one of the guys working on the air conditioner unit in here." I was hoping the man had something to munch on in his pockets because I didn't plan on sharing any of my food with him. Especially my drinks.

"Thank goodness, no patients or their families are in there with you."

"Yes, you're right about that. Sachs said he's working to get us, along with the other people on different elevators, out as soon as possible."

"Okay, hopefully, you'll get out soon. I've got to run. One of my patients is complaining about his catheter."

"Bye," we said in unison and hung up the phone.

I sat on the floor to make myself comfortable. Meanwhile, I started going through my cell phone to erase all of Tory's pictures.

"Do you mind if I sit down?" the man asked.

"Go ahead."

"By the way, my name is Vincent Rappaport. I go by Vince." He took his hat off and opened up his work jacket. He looked to be in his mid-thirties. Curly hair, dark-skinned, shaped-up beard, his rough hands made him appear like he worked hard. From the look of his body, working out seemed to be a priority.

"Well, you already know my name."

"Are you always this impatient and pessimistic?"

"It depends."

"According to the look on your face, this is the worst thing that could happen to you. You seem like the world is coming to an end just because the elevator has stopped."

"Yeah, pretty much."

"A few months ago, I saw you on the news about the pharmacist giving you the wrong prescription at Drug Aid. It's all over YouTube."

"I know."

"My sister thinks you're a hero for women around the globe. I just made a mental note to never get on your bad side if I ever met you."

"It would be wise to take your own advice about me."

We both started laughing.

"So what do you do at the hospital?"

"I'm a nurse practitioner and specialize in OB/GYN, but I can work any floor."

"Was it hard going through the nursing program?"

"Yeah, but I refused to give up and wanted to secure my future. Besides, my mother wouldn't have let me hear the end of it if I left school. She's been a nurse for the last twenty-five years. How long was your training for air conditioners and whatever else you do?"

"It was less than a year. I specialize in air conditioning, heating, as well as ventilation and refrigeration."

"How long have you been working for Air Professionals?"

"I started this company about nine years ago. To tell the truth, word of mouth and providing quality service has kept my business alive."

Servicing the hospital is probably a good size contract for him, I thought, impressed by his story. "I see."

Being in such cramped quarters, the heat was starting to get to me. I quickly pulled out my peach-flavored green teas and Pop-Tarts, handing Vince one of each.

"Thank you."

"No problem."

Suddenly, a dispatch came over to his walkie-talkie. "Vince, where are you, man? Do you want us to start the job without you?"

"Excuse me, Nya. Rodgers, go ahead and start the job. I'm stuck in an elevator. Hopefully, I will be there soon."

Then we heard over the intercom, "Folks, this is Sachs again. The fire department is here. It's going to be about two hours before we can get everyone out. Again, I apologize for the inconvenience."

"Is this going to kill your lunch plans with your husband?" he asked, obviously trying to find out whether I was married or not.

Shortly after returning home from my mom's house, I had taken my ring off and no longer wore it.

"No, it's not. My husband won't be meeting me for lunch or dinner. I am separated from him. He's an alcoholic and left me."

"Whoa! I'm sorry. I didn't mean to open up a wound for you. No wonder, the first time I noticed you in the hospital, you looked like you had a lot on your mind."

"It's all right. You didn't know."

For the next few hours, Vince and I talked. He told me plenty of funny jokes to pass the time. Before I knew it, we were out of the elevator. He went his way, and I went mine.

Chapter 33

While standing in line to pay for my gas at the gas station, I couldn't help but notice how the gas prices continued to fluctuate. This week a gallon was $3.40. Ten years ago, I remember filling up with up eighteen dollars worth of gas in my Toyota Corolla. Granted, my car now had a bigger gas tank, but I still felt like it cost me an arm and a leg just to fill up. Now I stopped at forty-five dollars, hoping that would get me as close to full as possible. Fortunately, the hospital was only a ten minute drive from my home.

Today's line was unusually long, and about seven patrons were talking about how pissed off they were to have to pay so much for gas. I wasn't purposely trying to be nosy, but I overheard the manager tell the cashier that their gas would run out by four o'clock this afternoon. Thankfully, I got my gas before the meltdown hit.

All over this area, gas stations were temporarily closing down due to insufficient gas. Daddy had often told Leah and I that the situation reminded him of the long gas lines back in the 1970s. I was wondering if the country was returning to those times.

As I was walking out of the convenience store wishing I had brought those hot and spicy flavored pork rinds, a voice blurted out, "Hey, Nya. I haven't seen you in a minute."

"Hmm. It's you."

I compared Charles to a broken-down car. If you don't do anything to fix it, then it will just sit there. He was still in the same position he was in right after high school—jobless, lazy, and not doing much of anything to get by on his own. He loved living at home with his mom. To him, living at his mother's house was a pure luxury, with three meals a day and clean clothes every week guaranteed to him. In his eyes, he was living the lifestyle of the filthy rich and famous. Honestly, it's a damn shame. Fortunately for me, I ran once I realized I was dating a loser.

A month ago, I saw his distraught mother in Food Lion. I was still her favorite. Maybe, she'd never accept the reality that her son did let me get away. She confessed Charles refused to get a job because he wanted to have his own company. He could at least fix things up around the house and take the trash out, but he didn't even do that, she complained.

It's so unfortunate how Charles' life turned out. He'd had one of the highest scores in the class on the SAT. I wondered what he could have been if he'd had more ambition and just applied himself better.

"You need me to pump your gas?" he eagerly asked.

"No, I already did, but thank you," I said, keeping my response to minimum. Every time I ran into Charles, he got delusional, thinking I would give him twenty minutes of my valuable time.

"How have you been?"

"I'm well." I nodded as I opened my car door. Charles wouldn't speak to me if Tory was here, since he knew a beatdown in the parking lot would be probable for him.

"With a face like yours, are you still getting away with everything?" he asked, a grin on his face.

"Yes, even murder. I'm warning you, don't get too close."

"I heard about what happened to your husband. Word gets around," he explained in an irritating tone.

Charles was bringing up the subject just to get a quick rise out of me. He was the type of man who loved it when women got mean with him.

It was as if my rejecting him many times over and over again made him want me even more. While sitting on his mother's couch watching music videos, was he cooking up the master plan to win me back? Charles had nothing to offer me or bring to the table, but yet somehow he felt as though he deserved another chance. Yes, I did believe in second chances, but with him, I definitely had to decline.

"Is that so?" I shot back at him, trying to keep my cool.

Today, I was leaving my anger, frustration, and self-pity party at home for the sake of my cute little goddaughter, Natalie, who'd landed the star role of Snow White in her school's play. Today was her debut performance, and I wasn't going to miss it for anything or anyone. Especially Charles, of all people.

"Yeah. Momma told me she ran into you at the store."

"Tell her I said hello. I've got to run," I replied, putting the key into the ignition.

"It was good seeing you. Maybe we could get together, you know, go to a late-night movie, just like old times."

"Sorry. At this time, I'm not giving out any samples." I drove off, leaving him looking stupid in my left rearview mirror.

"Cock-teaser!"

Chapter 34

Leah, Tara, Yvette, and I had attended the same school. Pulling up to the parking lot, I reminisced about our childhood there—the countless jump rope competitions we had during recess almost every day, the candy necklaces, Fun Dip, and Bubblicious bubble gum we all used to trade. Then there was the janitor, George Benson, who most of the kids feared. He used to walk the halls daring us to litter in "his" hallway.

Yvette stood up and motioned with her hand for me to join Jarvis, their son Michael, and her. "Glad you could make it." They had the look of proud parents on their faces. The dreadful mother-in-law was front and center in the auditorium. I cracked up laughing when Yvette mentioned to me that Grace had helped Natalie practice for hours on her lines like it was a Broadway show.

"I couldn't miss Natalie's first play," I told her after sitting down. Thankfully, I didn't forget the Sony digital camera to record the play. Next, Yvette's parents should show up.

"When is the show going to get started?" Leah asked after she found where we all were sitting.

Even at a child's school play, she dressed as if she was going to a club showing way too much cleavage I was quite embarrassed. If I knew one thing, she was definitely proud of what she had to show off.

"In about ten minutes," Yvette answered.

"Where's Tara?" I asked.

"I don't know," Leah said. "I texted her and left her a voice mail, but no answer."

"Shhh! Please be quiet," Grace said. "The show is about to start."

Grace refused to let anyone call her by her last name or put Mrs. in front of her name, claiming it made her feel way too old. But Leah and I were raised to show respect for our elders.

Little Natalie stole the show and, along with the other members in the play, received a standing ovation. Jarvis had white carnations for his baby. I had the *Snow White and the Seven Dwarfs* limited edition DVD to give to Natalie, which would make a great addition to her DVD rack. Afterward, we all stood in line to congratulate Natalie and give her lots of love. Instead of giving her a kiss, her baby brother Michael drooled on her. We all started laughing.

Since the middle of the show, my cell phone had been blowing up. I didn't even bother looking at the phone, thinking it was my job calling me. I needed a break.

"Hello?" I answered.

"Nya," Rob screamed on the phone.

"What's going on? Are you all right?"

"No. Tara was in a horrible car accident."

"Oh no! What hospital was she taken to?"

"She's at your hospital, Creekdale Memorial. I don't know what to do. What if the baby doesn't make it? Tara looks pretty banged. I can't lose her. I have Ryan with me, but he's getting restless. It's getting hard for me to keep it together."

I could hear the pain and anxiety in his voice. I wanted to cry, but I had to remain calm. I dealt with distraught families and friends almost every day at my job, but when it came to my friends and family, it was hard.

"Leah and I are on our way. I can get Leah to keep Ryan. I will be there no later than fifteen minutes." I hung up the phone and my heart began to race.

"Listen, Tara was in a car accident. She's at my hospital. We've got to get over there now," I said to everyone.

"What are the doctors saying?" Yvette asked.

"I won't know till I get there. All Rob said was that she looked banged up."

"Let's go," Leah declared.

"I'm going too." Yvette nodded her head.

"I understand if you don't want to leave Natalie on her special day," I said to Yvette and Jarvis.

"Tara is like a sister to me. She needs all three of us right now. Jarvis and Grace can take the kids home. Let me help him get the kids settled in the car. You go ahead. I'll be right behind you." Yvette threw Michael's bag over her shoulder and grabbed her keys out of her purse.

I couldn't get to the hospital fast enough. Pushing seventy-five on a fifty-five mile-per-hour highway, I didn't care. Getting to Tara was the only thing I could think about.

"How is she?" I asked Karen after barging into the emergency room doors.

"We're working her now. I got samples of her blood and took her blood pressure. Her reading is skyrocketing. We may need to take the baby."

"I want in," I demanded, quickly looking for scrubs.

"No, Nya, you're upset. You won't be any good to Tara in surgery."

"The patient's heart rate is dropping, and she is non-responsive," the attending doctor added, reviewing the monitor.

"Doctor, should I prepare her for surgery?" Karen inquired.

"Yes, she is approximately thirty-two weeks. We need to prep for a cesarean section."

Karen said, "Will you—?"

"Yes, I will let her husband know what's going on." I turned to run toward the patient waiting room.

For the next hour or so, I held Rob's hand and tried to keep him at ease. Yvette sat close to Tara's father and brother, who both put their heads down and began to pray. Honestly, I was scared myself.

According to the police report, Tara was hit pretty hard by a drunk driver and spun around Highway 264 before landing into a concrete wall. Anger surfaced within my chest. Another person's stupidity and irresponsibility may have killed one of my best friends. Every time anyone walked by with blue scrubs on, I was hoping it was Karen. Finally, she walked into the waiting area.

Before I could even get the words out of my mouth, Rob asked, "How is she?"

"Tara is stable. There appears to be no brain damage. We had to take the baby. Congratulations, Mr. Peters! You have a six-pound baby girl. Your wife is in the intensive care unit, and the baby is in the NICU unit. We want to monitor both of them for the next several days."

Rob didn't hesitate to hug Karen. Then he turned to me, Yvette, Leah, and his in-laws, and we all began to hug each other.

"Thank you so much," I whispered in Karen's ears.

"You're welcome," she replied.

"Tara and I finally decided the baby's name will be Victoria Mary Peters. When can I see both of them?" Rob asked Karen.

"You can see your daughter now. We're hoping Tara will wake up in the next couple of hours. Follow me so you can get to hold baby Victoria."

A couple of hours later, we all sat at Tara's bedside waiting and hoping for her to wake up. Yvette, Leah, and I were watching *The Wedding Date* on the television in her room.

Tara lifted her head and began looking around. "Where am I?"

Rob had gone to the check on the baby for the fourth time, and Tara's parents had gone down to the cafeteria to grab coffee, sodas, and snacks from the vending machine.

"You're in the hospital," Leah said to her.

"I remember the accident. Someone hit me," she said, placing her hand on her forehead. Just then, she gasped and clutched her stomach. "Oh my God! The baby! Where is she? Oh God! Is she okay?"

I moved her hands off her stomach. "Relax, honey. Victoria is fine."

"Is she healthy, with ten fingers and ten toes intact? How many pounds did she weigh?"

"Yes, the baby is healthy. She's premature and barely six pounds. That baby may be little, but she's a fighter just like her mother. Rob just went to check on her again. I believe your brother is with her too. She is so precious," I replied, holding her right hand.

"Has she been crying?"

"Yes, a little. I think she may be ready to breastfeed, if you're up for it. After the nurses took the necessary tests, I changed her and fed her formula. It's a good thing her auntie works in the hospital. Otherwise, they wouldn't have let me. Let me tell you, that girl has got a good grip on the nipple bottle. I can already tell she's going to love eating." I smiled.

"She's beautiful," Leah added.

Yvette had a huge smile on her face. "Victoria has your nose and eyes."

"It's going to take some time to really see who she will look like or if she will be a combination of Rob and you," I said.

"She's going to look like me, of course." Tara, weak from the surgery, was barely able to giggle.

Leah grinned. "I'm just grateful my club buddy made it through."

"Me too. I remember the accident." Tara took a deep breath. "As I turned the wheel to try to get control of the truck, it felt as if the devil and God were fighting over me. I'm here, I survived, and I want to see my baby."

Chapter 35

"Excuse me. I'm looking for Nya Sothers," a delivery guy said to no one in particular as Karen, Evita, Donna, and myself were scattered around the nurses' station.

"I'm Nya Sothers," I replied, waving my hand as we all admired the fruit basket from Edible Arrangements, consisting of strawberries, honeydew melon, watermelon, cantaloupe, and grapes.

"Ma'am, I just need you to sign this sheet for confirmation." The delivery guy pointed to his clipboard.

"Who are they from?" Donna asked.

He shook his head. "Unfortunately, I'm not authorized to tell you who sent them."

"Hmm. I don't know," I said, signing my name.

"Oh, Ms. Sothers, before I forget, here is a box of frosted blueberry Pop-Tarts and a case of green tea."

"Thank you." I nodded. *Wow! I never would have guessed the air conditioner man had given me a second thought.* This certainly brightened up my day.

"Read the card," Evita demanded.

"Nya, I enjoyed our conversation and wanted to return the favor of the light snack we ate in the elevator. If you want to continue our conversation, meet me at the March of Dimes walkathon. I'll be number 403. Have a nice day. Vince."

Karen, who was reading the note along with me, looking over my right shoulder, said, "Aaw, he's so sweet. I wish someone would do that for me. Nya, that man may be a keeper."

"I don't even know him. He's not on the good-guy list yet."

Donna asked, "Are you going?"

"Yes, I'll be there. I happen to be number 804. Now, let's go enjoy this fruit flower bouquet in the comfort of my office. Whatever we don't finish, I'll put in my miniature refrigerator and save it for tomorrow.

The rest of my day, I was feeling somewhat special that someone had cared enough to send me an edible arrangement.

Chapter 36

Mother Nature decided to be kind to us. The weather wasn't too hot, too cold, or too windy. As I approached the park, more and more people started gathering around waiting for the event to begin. I spotted Vince doing a few rounds of warm-ups and stretches before the walkathon. He was dressed in a black-and-gray jogging suit. I woke up this morning and decided to sport a light blue one with a white tank top.

"Good morning," I greeted him.

"Hey," he replied smiling. "Good morning to you too."

"Thank you for the edible arrangement."

"Since I didn't have your number, I figured I could have them deliver the fruit arrangements to your station. It was my way of saying thank you, and was long overdue.

"My coworkers and I ate from it for days. I really appreciate it, along with the green tea and the blueberry Pop-Tarts." I giggled.

"So you like to share with others. I'm learning something about you already."

"I guess you are. I love the ladies that I work with each day. I couldn't ask for a better team to run the hospital floors with." I nodded.

"I can tell you're different from other women, so I had to try a different approach. I didn't know you were sponsored to walk as well."

"Yes, along with hospital staff, family, friends and me, we all pitched in to help for such a worthy cause. I exceeded the goal of five thousand dollars and ended up raising about seventy-five hundred dollars."

"Ladies and gentlemen, thank you for taking the time to be with the March of Dimes organization today. We are very grateful and appreciate the time and effort our sponsors and many volunteers have put into this event to make it happen. We will begin in ten minutes. If you're walking, please be ready at the starting line, which is to my left." The announcer on a microphone pointed in the direction we needed to go.

"What made you get involved with the March of Dimes?" I inquired after the walk had begun.

"My mother drank alcohol while pregnant with my little sister. Needless to say, she was born premature. Thankfully, she had no birth defects and grew up as a normal kid. My mother finally kicked the booze after my baby brother came along, and she joined forces with the March of Dimes. That was twenty-five years ago. Ever since, my whole family has been involved. I usually give money, but this year, I wanted to walk as well. You know, it truly feels good to give and help others out. What about you?"

"This is my second year walking in the March of Dimes. I also enjoy raising awareness for this cause."

"Enough about me. Where are you from?"

"I was born and raised in Virginia Beach. That's right. I'm a beach girl to the fullest. I have a sister named Leah. She's only two years younger than me, and we're quite close. It's only the two of us. My parents decided not to have any more kids. I'm truly a daddy's girl at heart." I giggled.

"I'm originally from Kennesaw, Georgia. I'm the oldest out of the three of us. My brother and sister live in Atlanta, and I'm here all by myself."

"Why did you settle here?"

"Well, I went to school to study law at Old Dominion University."

"I graduated there with a nursing degree a few years back."

"I never graduated. College just wasn't for me."

"Well, it's not for everybody."

"After I left Old Dominion, I went back home to visit my parents. They were quite disappointed that I didn't complete my courses to get a degree, especially my mother. My father said, 'Boy, you got three options, which is the military, become a welder, or join the family business of heating and air.' I went to school, joined forces with my father, and twelve years later, my business is standing strong. My father taught me a lot about building strong business relationships. In fact, seventy-five percent of the business coming in is from word of mouth and referrals from people who have used my services and have been satisfied."

"How old are you?" I questioned, impressed with his last remark.

"I'm thirty-two. I'll be thirty-three in December." He nodded.

"This year, I turn twenty-nine in November. We're both late babies in the year."

"Is there anyone special in your life?"

"No, not at this time. It used to be my soon-to-be ex-husband. He and I were married for four years. We were happy." I wondered if I could handle divorcing him. *If I see him with another bottle in his hand, I would sign the dotted line on the divorce papers so fast.*

"What happened?"

"After his father died of a sudden heart attack, he took a turn for the worse and began drinking. In his mind, alcohol helped him cope better with the loss of his father. It consumed him and destroyed our marriage. I gave him an ultimatum. It was either me or the bottle. He not only left me, but he also left his tight-knit family. He left all of us. It's really taken a toll on his poor mother. It's ironic how both of us have dealt with loved ones and alcohol addiction."

"Yes, it is. Have you tried looking for him?"

"I have tried looking for him by going to the police and hiring a private investigators. Nothing has turned up. It's as if he's vanished with no trace, but I can only assume that's how he wanted it. Ten months and counting was the last time, I laid eyes on him," I vented, looking down.

Vince responded with a sympathetic tone. "That situation probably hurt you bad."

"Oh yes. I couldn't get out of bed for weeks. Then one day I decided that my husband had made his choice to ride off into the sunset with alcohol. Now, I'm making the choice to move on with my life. I often wonder why this has happened to me. I'm stronger now, but it damn sure knocked me down for a while. And I still wonder why I had to go through all this."

"I often wondered the same thing when I saw my mom trying to drink herself to death. The only advice I can give you from my experience is that when he finally chooses to stop drinking, he will, but it has to be on his terms."

"I suppose. Most times, still I fear the worst. For a while, every time my phone rang or the doorbell rang, I imagined it was a state trooper or police officer telling me that he'd died. He's put me through so much. I don't see myself ever being friendly or even cordial toward him."

"It took me many years to reestablish a healthy relationship with my mother. My sister had the most resentment. On the day she got her period, Mom was too busy drinking to take her to the drug store to pick up female products. Since my father was at work, I had to pick up the slack and take her. The girl I was dating at the time showed her how to use a maxi pad."

"That was noble of you," I said, impressed by him again.

"I'm very protective of my sister."

"Are you dating someone?"

"No, I'm not right now. I was married once. After Charlene, my ex-wife, found out that I left ODU, our relationship went into a downward spiral. To be honest, at heart, I'm just a plain old country boy, and she was a city girl. We just weren't compatible. She tried to change me, but it didn't work. Despite me paying every last bill in the house, it still wasn't good enough for her. After she finished up her degree at ODU, she became a court reporter. She kept nagging me about going back to school to be a lawyer. I told her so many times to stop trying to convince me because I wasn't going back. It put a severe strain on our marriage. Not to mention, her expensive lifestyle wasn't helping things either. Dining out all the time in expensive restaurants, shopping at high-end fashion boutiques, and desperately trying to keep up with the Joneses was all she cared about. It wasn't in my best interest to stay with her anymore. We've been divorced for three years. Now she sees I am successful and have my own business, she wants me to give the marriage another try. I don't want her back though. Ultimately, I know deep down she will never accept me for who I really am."

"Do you have any little ones running around?"

"No, I don't have any kids. One day, I wouldn't mind having a little Vince Junior watching television in the man cave with me."

"Is your man cave inside or outside of your house?" I asked, trying my best to keep a straight face.

"It's inside. I have a spare bedroom that I use. It's where I hold all my Pittsburgh Steelers gear—cups, T-shirts, jackets, raincoat, an umbrella, and a few posters."

I laughed. "You're definitely a fan."

"That's right. My whole family, we love our Steelers. What about you, Nya? Do you have any children?"

"Nope. It was in the plans, but things didn't work out that way."

Our conversation went everywhere, we talking about everything under the sun.

Before we knew it, the walk was over. Afterward, all walkers were treated to lunch, which consisted of turkey, ham, or roast beef sandwiches, Baked! Lays chips, a drink, and a chocolate chip cookie, courtesy of Quiznos. After getting our food, Vince and I huddled over to a nearby tree to sit down and eat.

"What plans do you have for the rest of the day?" he asked.

"I have a late shift tonight. One of the team members called out sick, and I'm on call today."

"I parked nearby. Are you?"

"No, the garage park is where my Camry sits."

"May I take you to your car?"

"Yes."

Vince led me to the direction of his vehicle. Once inside, he turned on his CD player and jazz music started playing

"Nice truck," I said, checking out his metallic GMC Denali.

"Thank you. I just got this not too long ago. It comes in handy when I'm lugging around parts."

"You're welcome. Hmm. So you're a jazz fan?"

"I'm a Miles fan. He's one of my favorites. If I'd had a trying day at work, I kick back, put on my iPod, and listen to the sounds."

"Make a right and my car should be on the left-hand side."

"Here we are. Thank you for coming out to walk with me. I enjoyed myself.'

"Likewise," I replied, a tad disappointed our time was up.

"Can I give you my number?"

"Sure. I'll you give mine as well."

Vince watched me get into my car. Next stop would be my house to take a hot shower and get a nap in before walking through those hospital doors.

Chapter 37

Vince had officially gotten the nice-guy title. It'd been five weeks and he'd been nothing but a gentleman to me. I looked forward to hearing from him. Due to our hectic schedules, we didn't get to talk every day, or every other day for that matter, but "good morning" text messages helped me through the day, and "sweet dreams" text messages sure helped me get through the night. These little things meant the most to me.

Lately, I'd been working a lot of overtime. Since foreclosed homes were on the rise and showing up everywhere in Virginia Beach, Norfolk, Portsmouth, Suffolk, and Chesapeake, where I lived, the property taxes on homes had skyrocketed. I was required to pay one hundred and fifty dollars more a month.

The paychecks from Tory's boss were due to run out soon. I couldn't blame him. He couldn't direct-deposit that check into our account forever. At the end of the day, Irv still had a business to run.

Pretty soon, I'd be paying the mortgage and the rest of the bills by myself. I refused to let the sheriffs put a padlock on my front door. Sure, I still had the cash tucked away securely into my safety deposit box, but I only wanted to use it for emergencies.

Tonight, I was hanging out with the girls down at the beach at a fairly new, exclusive club called the Skybar, located on top of the four-star Hilton Hotel. Since having the baby, Tara didn't go out at all, so she was very eager to get out tonight. She still had to prove to herself that she was still a showstopper. To flock to this club on a regular basis, membership was required, which cost a few hundred dollars. Luckily, I was able to nab free admission and VIP passes from a patient of mine who worked there.

Many people were standing in line hoping to get in. The four of us got to bypass everyone with our VIP passes. Inside the club, a tray giving the illusion of a burning candle first caught my eye. And the waitresses wore white dresses with ballerina shoes.

Next, I noticed two bars and two pools, but no one was in the pool, and people were standing around it. I didn't see any tables either. Instead, lawn chairs and exotic plants were laid out. The lights were an illuminating blue color, and people were lying down on king-size beds placed at each end of the club, sipping on their complimentary champagne. The beds replaced the VIP section.

We were definitely not going to be getting one of those beds tonight. Even with VIP passes, the price to sit or lie on one of those luxurious beds was one thousand dollars.

So many people were waiting on drinks from the bar, yet we were lucky enough that one of the waitresses was kind enough to take our drink orders from near the bed we were standing by.

The DJ played "Addiction" by Ryan Leslie, "Viva la Vida" by Coldplay, "American Boy" by Estelle, "Superstar" by Lupe Fiasco, followed by "Good Life" by Kanye West.

"Four people just got up from the chairs over there. Let's go sit down," I suggested before heading over there, trying to hurry up so we'd get there before anyone else.

"Ladies, I finally found you all. Here are your drinks." The waitress grinned. Good service was worth a twenty-dollar tip from me.

"Thank you," we all replied in unison.

"Paper Planes" by M.I.A. started playing. That was our cue to get on the dance floor.

Afterward, Leah attempted to get the DJ to play reggae, and he managed to find some tunes by Beenie Man, Sizzla, and Sean Kingston.

A woman tapped me on my shoulder. "Excuse me."

I turned around to face her. She looked to be in her mid-forties, and was well manicured and adorned in jewelry. "Yes?"

"My friend and I were just leaving. This bed cost me a thousand bucks, and I don't want it to go to waste. Your party is welcome to enjoy the rest of the evening on it."

"Thank you," I said, smiling.

"No. Thank you. On my way out, I'll let the waitress know you'll be taking it over. I know who you are."

"You do?"

"Yes, a while back, I saw you on the news about that scandal at Drug Aid. That pharmacist was a complete jerk. You definitely showed him. It empowered me. My friends and I couldn't stop talking about it for a week. I'm not a woman to reveal my age, but years ago, when I was starting out in the corporate world, my boss came on to me. I didn't report it. You've encouraged women all over the world to take a stand against sexual harassment. By the way," she yelled over the music, "I hope you know the news segment has been playing on YouTube.com."

"Yes, I'm aware of that." I smiled and nodded.

The night turned out great. We laughed, drank, and danced the night away. Leah and Tara, of course, were the center of attention. Leah was ecstatic to be able to party with her friend again, and Tara felt redeemed that, after becoming a mother, she still knew how to have fun and party.

Chapter 38

The two things I loved about Vince's house was the spacious three-piece sectional in the living room, and the home theatre. Nine years ago, he'd bought a foreclosed home in Virginia Beach. Vince showed me pictures of before and after the renovation. The previous owners had left with a bang, literally. There were countless holes in the walls, cabinets torn down, and the banister was missing from the staircase. Not to mention, their dog had urinated all over the carpet. It looked as if Vince gutted the whole house and started from scratch. I'm proud to say he'd done most of the work himself. I couldn't even take painting for five minutes without getting a nagging headache. I considered myself a diva, so no tool belt for me.

I was heading to his house when he called and asked me to meet him somewhere else. He was waiting for me at the door.

"Why did you have me meet you here?" I asked as I walked up the stairs toward the entrance of the building.

"I haven't told anyone this, but I'm taking courses here. I'm not a student at the Culinary Institute, but annually a class is offered and open to the public."

"You should have told me. I can help you cook."

"I'm sure you can, but a bachelor has got to learn on his own. One of the things I look forward to when visiting my hometown is Momma's cooking. Unfortunately, I can't bring her home with me, so I can't have her home cooking on a daily basis. One of the assignments is to invite someone to try a meal that you've prepared. The first person I thought of was you." Vince grinned.

"Aaaw, I'm honored. Show me the way," I said, walking into the building.

"Here is a list of each item you will taste. You must judge me on presentation, texture, and overall quality of the food."

"Will do." I nodded with a hint of excitement.

"How do you like your steak cooked? Rare, medium rare, or well done?"

Vince helped me into a chair. It wasn't part of the requirement, but I had to admit, I loved how I was being treated right now.

"Rare steak is going into the absolute danger zone for me. I prefer medium, please."

"Yes, ma'am."

Vince was a preparing fried mozzarella cheese sticks with a side of marinara sauce. He dropped the entire bag of cheese sticks on the floor. To keep from laughing, I bit my tongue. From the expression on his face, you would've thought the world was coming to an end.

The main course was a peppercorn-crusted steak, fried sweet potato fries with a honey-glazed sauce, and sautéed spinach with fresh onions and garlic. And dessert was the ultimate sugar delight. Vince dipped a Snickers bar in a sweet flour batter on a wooden stick and fried it. Once it came out of the fryer, he sprinkled powdered sugar on it and drizzled Hershey's Chocolate Syrup. I could have eaten the whole thing by myself.

"How did I do?" he asked after I handed his instructor the score sheet.

"Are you sure you haven't cooked before?"

"Yes." He nodded.

"You get an A plus, one hundred, or whatever the highest score can be. I could tell you were nervous at first. Eventually, you calmed down while preparing the food. Thank you for letting me take on the task of being your taste tester. More importantly, I appreciate the effort you put into it."

"You're welcome."

"Where to now?" I inquired as we walked out of the building.

"Since my house is closer, let's park your car there, and we can ride together to catch the ferry."

"All right, I will follow you."

The ferry ride took us to Norfolk, where we stayed for a little while and walked around.

"Can you believe the city of Norfolk could be considering tearing down Waterside?" Vince asked. "I saw an article in the paper about it."

"I wasn't aware of that. It has been around for ages. As a child, I remember coming here. There was a fudge station, and the employees would sing and pass out free samples to anyone who walked by. Plus, the main reason we came down here were for the crabs. Mommy taught my sister and I how to eat them here. There's a true art to eating them."

"A lot of people are in an uproar about this building closing down. I'm hoping the city of Norfolk will make Waterside a historic landmark."

On the way back to his truck, Vince held me close as we rode the ferry. To be honest, I hadn't felt this good in a long time. I felt like a teenager experiencing a new romance. I discovered no one else was on the ferry but us.

"Nya, I've really been having a fun time with you."

"Likewise." I sealed our agreement on the subject with a kiss. As I closed my eyes and continued to kiss him with my tongue, I began to fantasize about having sex with him.

Next thing you know, our hands began to explore each other's bodies. My hand found its way to his dick and started massaging it up and down. To my satisfaction, he was a size I could handle, and even bigger than I thought.

The ferry docked. It was time to get off.

"Touching time is over." Vince smiled as we walked back to the truck.

"Hmm. I don't like to be teased." I grabbed the keys from him.

Once we reached the truck, I quickly unlocked the back passenger door, and we climbed in. Within seconds, I took off Vince's jeans. We kissed as I scrambled to get my clothes off.

"Let me taste your lips."

"You want more of my lips?"

"Who said I was talking about those lips?"

"Oh, is that so, Mr. Rappaport? Don't worry, you'll get your chance."

Being this horny is a drug in and of itself. I quickly pulled his dick through the opening in his boxers, reached down, and slowly started sucking on the tip. I was sliding my left hand up and down his shaft while sucking on the tip, and massaging his balls with my right hand.

Vince moaned, "Yes!"

Vince didn't let me play with his dick for long. He turned me over to lie on my back and took off the rest of my clothes. "My turn now." He gently kissed my neck down to my soaking wet pussy, opening my legs to expose my clitoris. He acted as if he had found the jackpot.

While his tongue ran up and down my hot spot, I felt like I had just won the grand prize. Over and over again, we played a cat-and-mouse game of me sucking his dick and him making me even wetter with his tongue. By the time he placed his condom-wrapped dick into my pussy, we were both about to explode.

At first, gentle strokes came as he sucked on my breast, but I really was longing for those long, deep strokes.

Vince didn't disappoint me, and I closed my eyes as we came together. Afterward, we just lay there holding each other for a few minutes.

Vince scribbled on the fogged up back window, "I like you."

We both laughed and kissed again.

Wanting more, he took it a step further and discovered my G-spot again.

Coming the second time around was so intense, I couldn't even move. I was grateful tomorrow was my day off. Vince had definitely made up for the entire year I went without sex.

The next morning, we woke up in his bed snuggled up together.

"How did I get here?" I whispered.

"You fell asleep, so I carried you into the house. I wore you out." He gently laughed.

Then I started laughing. "I loved it."

"Let's go back to sleep. You're off today, but I have to be at a job site at one this afternoon." He kissed my ear softly. "I want to stay close to you for as long as I can."

Chapter 39

Another month of bliss and good loving had gone by. It wasn't just the actual physical act of sexual intercourse that I enjoyed; it was the intimacy and closeness we shared that had become the most important to me.

We were in Vince's basement. It was so spacious, it could be a mini apartment. He even had a spare refrigerator down here.

"Are you sure you're done playing?"

"Yeah, I'm sure. We played four games," I reminded him.

"Even though, it's a tie, I'm still the reigning ping-pong champion."

"For now. I may steal your title from up under you." I giggled as I headed over to the couch to sit down.

"Almost every time, we're together you have cherry passion Tic Tacs in your possession. What is it about those red and yellow candies you love so much?"

"Well, it's the taste and the crunch when I bite into them. Plus, they're refreshing and keep my mouth moist."

"You ate all of them."

"No, I didn't. Two of them accidentally fell on the floor."

We both started laughing.

I eyed his workbag on the floor. "What kinds of tools do you have?"

"All kinds. Go ahead and take a look." He handed me the bag.

It didn't take long to find the tape measure.

"Take your pants off," I ordered him.

"What?"

I grinned. "Oh, I forgot to say please."

"What do you have the tape measure in your hand for?" Vince took off his pants and boxer shorts.

"Would you ever wear briefs for me?" I asked as he stood in front of me.

"I don't think so. Breathing room is a must down there."

While he was talking, I got on my knees and started sucking his dick. When he was solid as a rock, I stopped and took the tape measure to see how long he truly was.

"Hmm, you're eight and a half inches. No wonder you have no problems hitting my spot."

I took off my clothes and motioned for him to lie back on the couch. It took mere seconds to get the condom on him. I straddled him and glided my pussy down on his dick, my nipples slow-dancing in his face as I went back and forth.

"Damn, it's just so good," he whispered. "I'm trying not to cum."

"Don't fight it." I picked up the pace. "Cum in me."

Soon after, Vince came.

"Nya, you gave me no other choice," he said, wiping the sweat off his forehead.

I knew my pussy was good when I could make a man cum against his will.

Chapter 40

"How are things at home?" I asked Yvette as we were waiting for Tara to come back with the food.

She had left me with baby Victoria so she could run some errands and pick up the food. I was hoping she'd remember to pick up a pulled pork sandwich with special sauce for me. Tonight, we were having Frankie's ribs. She ordered barbecued beef and pork ribs, brown-sugar baked beans, potato salad, fresh made coleslaw and French fries. I made sure to bring a roll of dental floss. The worst feeling in the world was to have food stuck in between my teeth. For dessert, I gave Tara a hand and picked up apple tarts from Panera Bread. I was going to pile smooth whipped cream on mine.

"I'm hungry," Leah blurted out. "Tara needs to hurry back. Let me hold the baby."

"I have an announcement," Yvette said with excitement. "Grace is moving out. I repeat, the nosy mother-in-law is finally packing her bags."

"Wow!" I replied in disbelief. I thought she would never leave.

"Nya, I sort of took your advice."

"I reclaimed my house. For instance, one night I made spaghetti and specifically put oregano and garlic powder into the entire batch. Grace's stomach doesn't agree with it. Needless to say, she became sick with gas, diarrhea, and nausea. Once she and Jarvis confronted me, I acted as if I didn't know it would make her sick.

"Then I've been encouraging Jarvis to have his buddies over to watch the games more than usual. They're loud, and we all know Grace can't take a lot of noise, especially at night. Now it's Michael and his play dates. When the kids are done playing, books and toys are scattered all downstairs. One day she tripped on one of his toys and fell, and her butt and back was sore for days.

"But here's what broke the camel's back. I've been getting up an hour earlier at seven o'clock and blasting the radio on 95.7 in the morning to hear *The Steve Harvey Show*. She's a light sleeper, so once the program wakes her, most mornings she can't go back to sleep.

"Last month, when I invited the three of you over to the house, our laughing and joking around got on her nerves. She thought it was rude and inconsiderate toward her to have guests till midnight. I simply told her, 'This is my house, and I damn sure don't need your permission to do anything. If you don't like it, there's the door.' She's officially leaving." Yvette grinned.

"I know you're happy," Leah added, rubbing Victoria's back.

Just then Tara walked in. "Traffic is horrible." She put the food on the island in the kitchen.

"Fix me a plate," Leah said. "I'm starving."

"Go fix your own plate," I told her. "Give me the baby back. I can't get enough of holding her anyway."

"Did your three godmommies take good care of you?" Tara whispered to Victoria, who was falling fast asleep.

"Yes, we did," I reassured her. I gently placed the baby on her side in the playpen for a nap.

"Where's Ryan?" Leah asked. "He's so cute."

"Rob took him out to get a haircut and run a few errands. Plus, he wants to give me time with you all for a girls' night. Nya, I didn't forget your pork sandwich."

"Thank you. I'll take it home with me for a late-night snack or lunch for tomorrow. How are you feeling? No baby blues, right?"

"Mom's birthday was two days ago. I admit I was a little down, but in my heart, I know she's watching over the baby and me. At times, it's almost as if I can feel her presence in Victoria's nursery room."

"Maybe she's trying to let you know she's here," Yvette agreed.

"Yes, I second that notion," I added.

By now, we all were all huddled over the kitchen island.

"Me too." Leah took a bite into a rib.

"I've been seeing someone. Leah, pass me the coleslaw."

Yvette stopped pouring the cranberry-flavored ginger ale in her glass, and Tara suddenly looked at me.

Leah gawked at me with a look of disbelief. "It's about time, miss goody two shoes."

Yvette got right down to the nitty-gritty. "How long has this been going on? What's his name? Where is he from?"

"You must really like this guy to stray away from Tory." Tara shook her head, placing a few scoops of baked beans on her plate. "I didn't think you would ever get over him."

"His name is Vince Rappaport. He runs a heating and air conditioning business. He's from Kennesaw, Georgia. I've been seeing him for at about three months now."

"Why didn't you tell us earlier?" Tara questioned.

"I didn't know if it would last or if I would even like him. I didn't want to say anything about him until I was sure I liked him."

"Where did you meet him?" Yvette asked.

"Nya, before you say a word, I bet anyone a hundred dollars to pay my cell phone, it was at the hospital." Leah looked around for any takers.

"Yes, it was there." I nodded.

"I knew it. Nya, your name should be changed to Hermit Crab, because you don't ever come out to play anymore." Leah laughed.

"I've been busy with the hospital. Sick people need to be taken care of. On my days off, I have to help maintain the restaurant with Rome. I can't desert him like Tory did. He put most of his liquid assets up to get the business off the ground."

"Are you happy?" Tara asked.

"Most definitely so." I giggled.

"That's all that matters to me."

"Did you two have sex yet?" Yvette asked.

"Uh huh. It was so good."

"I'm happy for you." Yvette hugged me.

Then Tara hugged me next.

"Well, well . . . Hermit Crab is happy and getting some dick. After I eat a second plate,

I'm going to be ready for dessert. What are we having?"

"Apple tarts," I told her. "I'm warming them up in the oven."

Afterward, we played Monopoly. Next, we watched a movie called *The Best Man*. I could it watch over and over again.

Finally, we watched *Inside Man*.

Chapter 41

In his spare time, Vince played in a basketball league. At least twice a month, I was sitting up high in the bleachers to watch him play. His team was two games away from the championship.

Once I found out he played ball, I started watching ESPN to learn a little bit about the sport, which wasn't as complicated as I thought. I learned even more when watching games together with him.

Today a guy from the opposing team accidentally elbowed him on the back of his head, and he fell and busted his face against the floor. Blood began gushing down his face.

One of his team members punched the guy that elbowed Vince. Then the referee tried to intervene and ended up getting knocked down to the floor. Then, almost all of the players from both teams started fighting.

It was disgraceful to see grown men beating on each other, some of them, their children sitting on the bleachers watching it all happen.

Tomorrow, most of these guys are going to regret their actions.

I saw Vince go to a side bench and sit down. I quickly ran to his side. If anyone dared to hit me, they were going to get hosed down with the pepper spray sitting in my handbag.

"Is it bad?" he asked, looking up at me.

"It looks as though you're going to need stitches."

"Let's go to the hospital."

"There's no need for that place or an urgent care facility. I can stitch you up in no time. It's one of the luxuries of being with a nurse practitioner. Everything I will need is at my house. Can you walk? Do you feel dizzy?"

"I can make it up and walk. Yeah, I do feel somewhat dizzy."

"Please walk slow. When we get back to the house, I'll definitely take good care of you."

Putting in the stitches was a little bit painful for Vince. We got into a hot shower together, and I washed him up.

Pasta salad with grilled chicken, carrots, green and black olives and broccoli was waiting for us in the refrigerator.

Once I gave him two capsules of Tylenol PM, it only took fifteen minutes for him to fall asleep.

In the meantime, I caught up on laundry and shredding documents. One of my worst fears was having my identity taken from me, so I always made sure to shred any excess paperwork.

Hours later, sifting through my desk drawers, I found a picture of Tory and I with the whole gang. It was at Natalie's baby christening. *Today's our anniversary*, I thought as the tears flowed down my face. *How could he just stop caring and loving me?* It still hurt.

I headed to the living room, hoping television would lift my spirits a little.

"What are you watching?" Vince asked, coming into the living room. He sat right next to me.

"This show called *Dexter*," I quickly blurted out. I was hoping my tears had dried up. "I love it."

"I've never heard of it."

"It's about a guy who saw his mother get murdered at a very young age. From that experience, he has the urge to kill, but only bad people. As a trophy, he keeps a small amount of their blood on a slide. It's so raw, powerful, and intoxicating. I rented season two on Netflix. Unfortunately, for me, I had to wait two days for the DVD to arrive in the mail. I couldn't wait that long. After calling three Wal-Mart stores in the area, I found out the Battlefield Boulevard store had two copies of the second season left. I drove out there and purchased the DVD."

"Whatever Nya wants, she gets. You are so determined. It's one of the things I love about you. Plus, you're a hard worker, kindhearted, know how to move that ass, and can cook a decent meal." Vince kept his stare on me. "Have you been crying?"

"A little."

"What's wrong?"

"Nothing. How are you feeling?"

"Other than my head feeling sore, I'm fine. What about you?"

"Today would have been Tory and I's anniversary."

"I'm so sorry."

I buried my head in his lap. I needed a few minutes to get my emotions together.

"Where do I stand with you, Nya?" Vince asked after *Dexter* went off.

"What do you mean?"

"I'm divorced, you're not. If I even start talking about love, you change the subject. Am I just the rebound guy while you wait for your long-lost husband to possibly turn back up?"

"He's not coming back," I snapped back and got up to walk away.

"You say the words, but can you understand them? Right now, today, if he came back, who would you choose?"

"I don't know."

"Have you looked into starting divorce proceedings? The lawyer I used was very resourceful. I can give you her office number. With Tory being MIA, it won't be a sticky situation."

"Thank you for the advice and the offer. When I'm ready, I will start divorce proceedings on my own." I headed to the kitchen for a glass of water, my mouth feeling dry. I wasn't prepared for this conversation.

"Nya Sothers, I love you!" Vince declared at the top of his lungs.

I stopped dead in my tracks. Chills went down my spine. I didn't know what to say.

"Do you love me? I just want the truth. Please, no bullshit."

"I care a lot about you. I didn't expect any of this to happen, or for things to get this deep between us."

"Neither did I, but it happened, and we need to deal with it."

Now I was sorry I had told him today was my anniversary. "Vince, what do you want from me?"

"Your heart. At times, I feel like your body is here but your mind is somewhere else. You use work as a coping mechanism for what Tory did to you. I don't want to lose you, but I can't be with you unless some things change. I feel like I'm in competition with a man that isn't even here. We fit good together, but I need more of a commitment from you. No pressure," he said, coming toward me. "Just think about us really being together."

We were about to hug, when suddenly my cell phone rang. I looked at the caller ID before answering.

"Hey, Nelson. How's she doing?"

Leah had gotten her wisdom teeth removed last week and wasn't recovering well. I had called Nelson earlier to check on her and left him a message to call me back.

"Her fever won't break. I've been giving her Tylenol, but her temperature won't go down."

"Call the orthodontist and tell him she needs to go in for an emergency visit. I'll meet you at his office." I hung up the phone.

"Do you want me to tag along?"

"You don't have to, if your head is still hurting. Do you really feel up to it?"

"I got a pretty good amount of sleep. I feel like I could stay up all night. Besides, it gives me a chance to finally meet your sister." Vince smiled.

"All right." I grabbed my car keys from the table in the foyer.

It turned out Leah's crazy behind wasn't following the doctor's orders. Instead of light liquids and soft foods, she'd been eating fried chicken and drinking soda and had not been using the squirt instrument to get the excess food out from the holes. Now, she got a nasty infection and dry sockets.

The orthodontist cleaned out Leah's mouth. He also started her on antibiotics and gave her a stern talk about the seriousness of following doctor's orders.

"I feel good as new," Leah announced.

"You're going to follow what the doc says this time."

"Yeah, yeah," she responded, waving her hand at Nelson.

"The nurse is coming to bring you a cup of lime-flavored Jell-O," I informed her.

"Thanks for coming. I didn't want to worry your parents."

"I appreciate you not calling them," I said. "Mommy has a tendency to overreact, and I didn't want either of them to worry."

"Nya, you can shut your trap now. Step aside. You must be Vince. I hear you're making my sister happy. Keep it that way so she can stay the hell away from me."

Vince grinned. "Leah and Nelson, it's nice to meet both of you."

"Since you're not at death's door, we're going to leave. Call me if you need me to bring oatmeal over."

"Yuck! I hate oatmeal."

"I know, but it's one of the few things you can eat right now."

"Instead, bring me a takeout order from that restaurant you partly own. Which means I get it for free. I'm family."

Leah is definitely showing her behind tonight. Maybe, it's the antibiotics. "I'll think about it."

"You own a restaurant?" Vince asked after we stepped out of the elevator to head to the car.

"Yes, I do, but not by myself. Originally it was a business venture my husband started with his college friend Rome. When Tory's father died, he stopped doing much of anything. The restaurant was up and ready to open, so I took his role. I came on board to help out, paying the bills, running the payroll, and making sure taxes are being paying properly. Now, I truly understand why people dread the Internal Revenue Service.

Plus, I also help Rome in the creative aspect of things. He and I are constantly brainstorming for fresh ideas to help business grow. With Tory being gone so long, Rome and I decided to do the proper paperwork to remove him and officially put me as the second owner."

"I see." Lines started appearing across Vince's forehead. "When were you going to tell me?"

Vince's aggravation was beginning to rub off on me.

"What the hell is wrong with you?"

"It's everything with our whole situation. I feel as if you're so secretive about Tory. I've opened up my entire life to you."

"Listen, I try to put myself in another person's shoes. I know you don't always want to hear about my deadbeat bottle-sucking husband and what we have together. That's why I try not to discuss it. I know I don't want to hear about your ex-wife Charlene all the time. There is a thin line between venting and constantly talking about an ex. I don't want to cross any lines."

"Nya, you said *have*."

"What?" I snapped.

"You said, what we *have* together, referring to you and Tory."

"I didn't mean it like that." I sighed, shrugging my shoulders.

"Nya, I love you so much. I can't change your past or what was done to you. That's over and done with. What I can do is help change your future for the better. I'm willing to do everything in my power to make things work between us, so we can have a wonderful life together. But, at the same time, I refuse to sell myself short. Hell, you're not even divorced yet. You haven't even started the process. I think it's because you're not ready to let go of him. I need someone who's going to be totally committed to me. I'm sharing your heart in this relationship." Vince huffed. "I think we should stop seeing each other."

Chapter 42

As I walked down the hall, I heard someone crying in the nurses' locker room. I had just finished up one of my classes. I usually taught one class every other semester. I was glad I was teaching this semester because it kept my mind off everything going on in my personal life.

"Andrea, is that you?"

"Yes, it's me." Her face was bright red, and she was in desperate need of a tissue. Luckily, there was a box near one of the sinks. She took a few tissues to dry her eyes and wipe her nose.

"What's going on?" I asked, hoping she would open up to me. All the students knew I had an open-door policy.

"I can't do this anymore. It's too much to handle. I'm quitting today."

"How is this too much to take?"

"First of all, with the exception of you and two other nursing instructors, the rest of them are mean and hateful. I feel as though they come here just to torture us and make our lives hell. I have to put up with pure torture. This morning, Mrs. Kinmore made me feel stupid in front of the whole class. While doing my clinical, I forgot two of the twenty steps when administering medication to the patient. She went off on me, saying, if I wasn't willing to put the work in to learn all the steps, then I should look into an easier profession."

"I know Mrs. Kinmore can be a lot to deal with, but she's only trying to make you the best nurse you can be. She's pushing you because you have what it takes to be a registered nurse."

"Can you talk to her for me?" she pleaded.

"No, I won't do that. But I'll give you some advice though.

"Okay." Andrea continued to dry her tears.

"How long are you going to have to deal with Mrs. Kinmore and the other teachers you seem to despise?"

"Five months."

"All right then. Five months is not a long time. Kill those instructors with kindness and do what you're told. Some just want to see if you're going to crack. As a nurse, you will be put in stressful situations, with doctors and patients' families screaming at you. Mrs. Kinmore and the others are simply trying to prepare you for it. If you quit now, you'll always wonder what could have been. Don't take the easy way out. Besides, Andrea, you've come too far and worked too hard to get to this point with only two semesters left."

"Mrs. Sothers, you're right. I've got a lot of thinking to do."

"You're way much stronger than you think. Why don't you get yourself together and go down to the cafeteria and pick up one of those IZZE drinks I always see you with. Think about what I said. I hope it helps."

She grinned. "I will. Thank you."

"You're welcome. I hope to see you tomorrow." I walked out of the locker room hoping my words got through to her. *If Andrea decides to stay, in time, she'd be a hardworking nurse.*

Chapter 43

Leah was pushing her hand against my leg as she leaned over me, trying to reach her purse under my seat.

I hollered, "Leah, would you hurry up!"

"I got it!" she exclaimed as she pulled her purse out. "I have to make sure my makeup still looks fresh," she said with an attitude.

Who the hell tries to look cute and sexy going to the Pungo Strawberry Festival?

We were taking the little ones strawberry picking. Yvette decided it would be easier for all of us to pile us into the "mommy mobile," her Honda Odyssey.

"Are we there yet?" Michael, Natalie, and Ryan kept asking after only half an hour of being on the road. They had just finished watching a *SpongeBob* DVD.

Thank God, Yvette had a DVD player installed in the car. That helped the ride go a little smoother.

"One episode of *Go, Diego, Go!* and *Backyar-digans*," Yvette responded.

It had been years since I last went to the Strawberry Festival. I was curious to see how different it was going to be from the way I'd remembered it.

On the way there, Leah couldn't stop admiring herself in the mirror.

While Tara was giving Victoria a bottle, the kids were fighting over cinnamon-flavored Teddy Grahams. Yvette looked happy, like she didn't have a care in the world.

Seeing that, I decided to tune everyone out and take a nap until we got there.

"Remember, kids, stay with the group. Each one of you has whistles around your necks. Only whistle if you're in trouble or see 'stranger-danger.' If you're caught whistling for no reason, you won't get the grand prize." One by one, Yvette rubbed their hands with hand sanitizer and sprayed them down with bug repellent.

The grand prize was a magic show at the end of the day.

After washing some strawberries with water, we found a table and enjoyed the fruits of our labor.

We'd been picking strawberries for at least three hours. The strawberries were so sweet and fresh.

Eventually, all of us wanted real food. The kids settled for hotdogs, French fries, and a strawberry milkshake topped with whipped cream. Before they touched their food, Yvette advised them to have a bathroom break and wash their hands.

Yvette and I had sweet Italian sausages. For a snack, I had my eye on a crisp funnel cake topped with powdered sugar and strawberry puree. Tara and Leah chomped down on huge smoked turkey legs.

Afterward, we took the kids down to the local carnival. The three of them were very good throughout the day, so as promised, we took them to the carnival magic show to be entertained by clowns, animal-shaped balloons, face painting, and carousel rides. Victoria, too little to enjoy any of the fun activities, was napping in her stroller. *Next year will be different for her*, I thought.

The day was coming to an end. We were sitting at a picnic area set up adjacent to the strawberry fields. Yvette, Tara, Leah, and I were sitting at a picnic table while the kids ran around and played.

"Yvette, what did you use for your stretch marks after you had the kids?" Tara asked. "I have these stretch marks on my stomach that are not coming off. I've tried shea butter and olive oil, but it doesn't work for my skin."

"With Natalie, I didn't get any stretch marks. When I had Michael, my stretch marks looked more like battle scars. I used Bio-Oil. It should be coming to drugstores near us soon. Right now, you can only get it online at Amazon.com. I just ordered two bottles. You can have one, and hopefully, it will get rid of the stretch marks you have."

"Thanks, girl. The only thing left to deal with is my small pudge."

"Exercising is no fun," Leah said, joining in on the conversation.

"I second that notion." Yvette nodded.

We all began laughing.

Tara moved the conversation in the direction of my upside down love life. "So have you talked to Vince?"

"No, it's been two weeks," I revealed in between taking bites and slurping my strawberry and lemon-flavored snow cone. I felt as though my heart was at odds between Tory and Vince.

"Maybe he's giving you space and time to decide," Yvette said, keeping a close eye on the kids.

"I don't know what to do."

"Are you truly ready to move on with your life, or are you still carrying a torch for Tory?" Leah asked, pinning her hair up.

It was a hot and humid evening, and each one of us had our own portable fans blowing.

"We're thirsty," the kids announced after running over to us.

"Drink water." Leah handed them a cold bottle.

"I think I'm ready to move on. I'm still sad about how things turned out. Not knowing what happened to him is hard."

"Yeah, you're right. I can't imagine how difficult it must have been for you to lose him just like that." Tara shook her head. "When Tory left, you were at your lowest point, but you can't be moping around forever."

Yvette added, "Not knowing what's going to happen in the future can be fearful. Vince is brand-new territory, and you are probably scared to get into another relationship after Tory."

"You can't blame him for how he feels though," Leah pointed out. "I'm surprised he stuck it out for as long as he did. But you were honest with him from the beginning. I gotta give you credit there. The average person would have lied and not been truthful about how they felt."

On the way home, the kids were fast asleep, including Victoria. The van was calm and peacefully quiet.

Yvette slid Norah Jones' first album in the CD player. It was just what I needed to relax.

Chapter 44

I took a deep breath and reluctantly knocked on the door. It required a lot of courage to let go of the past and embrace the future.

Vince opened the door. "Hey. Come in."

"Hi," I replied back before walking into the house.

He led the way into the kitchen and sat down at the table.

"Thank you for seeing me."

He nodded, all eyes on me. "You wanted to talk and I'm going to listen."

"Last week I went to see a lawyer. He started the separation papers for me." I pulled a copy of the documents out of my purse and handed them to him.

Ms. Stein, my former manager at BankFIRST, went through a nasty drawn-out divorce. Needless to say, she came out on top. I just wanted what was due to me. She'd recommended Paul Goodman.

I didn't feel comfortable using Vince's lawyer, afraid that she'd violate our confidentiality and run her mouth to him, since I didn't know how close he was to his lawyer.

"You did?"

"I needed some time to think. Even though I'm scared about us and what tomorrow will hold, the truth is, I don't want to lose you. I want to let you inside my heart. Will you give me another chance?"

He shook his head. "I—"

"Before you go any further, I get the point." I walked out of the kitchen and headed for the door, trying hard not to shed a tear.

"Nya, wait, please." Vince chased after me and stopped me at the staircase banister.

"I can take the hint. You don't want me!"

"Shhh! You didn't even let me speak. I was shaking my head in disbelief because I didn't think you would actually go through with getting the divorce started. All I wanted from you was a little effort. These papers are a step in the right direction for us to be together. I want you back. I missed the hell out of you. The first couple of days I couldn't go to work because I felt so awful. The jazz music of Miles Davis couldn't even cheer me up."

"I missed you too."

"I'm scared about what the future holds too. Let's be scared together and get through it," he said, looking into my eyes.

We started kissing and fell into each other's arms on the staircase.

Vince pulled down his jogging shorts and boxers down to his ankles. Then he took off my shirt and lifted my skirt up. With his right hand, he pinned my hands to the staircase, and he ran his tongue against my breast.

It felt good to be at his mercy. I motioned for his dick to slip in between my moist pink walls. Every stroke was long, hard, and deep.

After cumming, we lay at the bottom of the staircase holding each other. It felt right being in his arms again.

He lifted me up and carried me to his bed, where we talked for hours, catching up on the last two weeks. I felt as though I had my friend back as well as my lover.

"I brought your favorite." I ran downstairs wearing Vince's robe to grab my purse.

"What is it? I love surprises," he inquired when I walked back into the bedroom.

"Before coming here, I stopped by Sugar Plum Bakery and picked up an assortment your taste buds will love. One of the things we have in common is a gigantic sweet tooth."

"Yeah, that's true." Vince grinned, looking through the box of cookies.

Inside was chocolate chip walnut, white chocolate macadamia, fudge, shortbread, rainbow, snicker doodles, oatmeal raisin, and gingerbread cookies. I couldn't resist grabbing two caramel glazed brownies.

While we were stuffing our faces, Vince popped a movie called *Inkwell* in the DVD player. It was so funny, I almost choked on a walnut. Vince and I got a good night's rest relieving all that tension.

Chapter 45

Yvette and Jarvis decided to cash in one of those babysitting coupons I'd given them. While Natalie and Michael stayed the night with me, their parents went to a concert at the NorVa, featuring The Roots and Chrisette Michele. The first gift Jarvis ever gave Yvette when they'd first started dating was a cassette tape of The Roots' first album, which she still had. Her favorite songs were "Silent Treatment" and "Proceed."

The next morning, after the kids got up and ate breakfast, we were out the door to run errands. As we sang the theme song to *Dora the Explorer* over and over again, we went to the restaurant then made the daily deposit at the bank.

Afterward, we were off to Wal-Mart to pick up a few items I needed. At this particular Wal-Mart, there was one way in and one way out. On the weekends, various security guards had to direct traffic to avoid accidents. Luckily, I beat the crowd and managed to get out of the parking lot without a fifteen-minute wait in traffic.

Our last stop was my parents' house. They had grown very fond of Natalie and Michael. Deep down, I think they secretly desired for Leah and I to push out some grandbabies of their own. After Mommy gave them tropical-flavored Fruit Roll-Ups, she became their new best friend.

By early evening time we were back at my house. I was helping Natalie to stir the saucepan.

She asked, "Auntie Nya, how long will the marshmallows take to melt?"

"It will only take a few minutes."

I clapped to praise Michael after he poured the box of Rice Krispies cereal in the buttered pan. The kids and I had fun as we mixed the cereal and melted marshmallows together. While we were making the treats, they couldn't help but lick their sticky fingers.

An hour later, Yvette and Jarvis arrived, just in time to enjoy what the kids had made.

"Nya, thank you so much for watching our little rug rats," Jarvis said, holding both of them in his arms.

"Thanks, sweetie." Yvette hugged me.

Thirty minutes after they left to go home, my cell phone rang.

"How's work?" I asked Vince after picking up the phone.

"We finished early."

"Great. Do you want to come over and lick Rice Krispies Treats off of me?"

"Hmm. That's sounds good, just as long as you let me lick it off your pussy."

I giggled. "I'll think about it."

"Are you still off all of next week?"

"Yes, I have a lot of vacation hours still left. Instead of cashing them in, this year I actually wanted to take the time off."

"You'll be happy to know that I'm taking off too. Pack your bags. We're going on a trip. Don't ask where. It's a surprise. It'll be good for us to get away. Plus, I'm getting hard just thinking I'll have you all to myself for an entire week."

"When are you picking me up?"

"I will be at your front door tomorrow morning around nine o'clock. I'm tying up a few loose ends. See you later."

Chapter 46

Besides my ears constantly popping, the flight was bearable. Chewing gum helped and I made sure to bring along my iPod. Vince slept during the entire flight and missed out on the tasty snacks the flight attendants gave away. I finally got a chance to listen to the complete album of a singer named Adele. Donna had recommended her album a few months ago, and I'd been a fan ever since. She and I both liked "Daydreamer" and "Make You Feel My Love."

Even though, we would be gone for five days, I'd packed enough clothes for ten days, which was only a mere three suitcases.

Vince couldn't get enough of the Viva La Juicy fragrance I was wearing. For the first time, in a long time, I felt totally at ease with my life.

"Where are we heading to?" I anxiously asked after arriving at the Atlanta airport and picking up the Honda CR-V at the rental car center. Did he really think I wasn't going to try asking at least one more time?

"You'll see." He grinned as we pulled out of the parking lot.

The staff at downtown Atlanta's W Hotel was courteous and professional with Southern charm and hospitality. Our hotel room looked fresh and clean, and had an urban oasis theme. And the view of the many skyscrapers surrounding us were breathtaking.

"I love the room. I appreciate you taking me away," I announced, lying on the bed.

"Me too. It's way too early to go to bed. You've still got the rest of the day ahead of you."

I sprung up from the bed. "I'm ready."

"At home, you break your neck to watch the National Geographic channel, so I figured you would enjoy Zoo Atlanta." He turned onto Cherokee Avenue.

When Ne-Yo's song, "She Got Her Own," popped on the radio, he started serenading me. I couldn't help but laugh.

With the digital camera and zoo map in my left hand, and Vince holding the other hand, we started off on the grand tour. All of the volunteers I stopped were kind enough to answer the many questions I had.

When we arrived there, the skies were gloomy, but the day turned out to be bright and sunny. This zoo was much larger than the Norfolk Zoo. The highlights of the tour were the African lions, rhinoceroses, giraffes, clouded leopards, flamingos, and king vultures. We learned that the black mamba, Aruba Island rattlesnake, and the bushmaster were the most venomous snakes. Even with them caged up, I was still frightened by them.

To cool down from the heat, we snacked on Edy's all natural lime-flavored Fruit Bars.

The last thing we did was ride the Georgia Natural Gas Blue Flame Express. I had no idea what Vince had next on the agenda.

It turned our Vince was paying attention when I mentioned to him a while back that I had never been skating. He took me to a beautiful outdoor skating rink. We skated quite a few laps around the rink, and I only had two falls. Not bad for my first time. Vince kept showing off his skills and didn't fall once. The two times I fell was because I was trying to avoid running into another person.

Once reaching Kennesaw, Georgia, I had a taste for chicken and steak fajitas. We decided to eat a late dinner at El Nopal Mexican Family Restaurant and head back to the hotel for some much-needed sleep.

The next day we rode down to the Kennesaw Civil War Museum and the National Battlefield Park. With Vince's passion for history, he was eager to tell me one of America's most cherished railroad stories, surrounding the date of April 12, 1862.

Since we were in his hometown, Vince showed me his elementary, junior high, and high school.

"Whose house is this?" I inquired as he pulled up to a beautiful two-story house.

"It's my parents' house. I want you to meet them," he said, getting out of the car.

Before I could get a word in, Vince's brothers, Howard and Stuart, were coming over to the car to welcome me. Mr. and Mrs. Rappaport and Beverly, his baby sister, all stood on the porch. Vince's best friend, Gary, and his two sons stopped by to visit. I had to admit, these folks were so friendly, the way they opened up their home to me. Pictures of their childhood and older generations all hung on the wall leading up the stairs for display. It was interesting to get a glimpse of Vince's great-great-grandfather. He looked just like him.

Mrs. Rappaport and Beverly whisked me away to play bingo. It was my first time. Luckily, I won two hundred and fifty dollars. Since they taught me how to play, I split it three ways with them.

After we got back to the house, Mrs. Rappaport wasted no time putting an apron on my waist to help prepare dinner. Fried chicken, fried catfish, string beans, corn on the cob, mashed potatoes, and coleslaw were on the menu. For dessert, handmade apple dumplings were turning golden brown in the oven. Mrs. Rappaport made it a point to cook everything from scratch.

"Make sure you come back," Vince's parents said, as they and the rest of his friends and family hugged me good-bye.

"What did you think about them?" Vince inquired, jumping on the highway.

"Your friends and family are wonderful people. They truly love you. As far as what I think about the stunt you pulled today, you're a jerk. It was wrong."

"Huh?"

"Vince, you put me on the spot with no regard to my feelings. We never discussed meeting your family. From visiting the museums and going to the schools, I felt raggedy. When you meet someone's parents, you have to mentally prepare yourself and make sure you look your best. If I knew, I wouldn't have come in jeans and a shirt."

"Nya, you definitely made a good impression. Don't worry about you being sweaty. All I wanted you to do is be yourself," he assured me with a slight grin shaking his head.

"It's not funny. I don't know what you told your parents about me, or my situation with not being divorced yet. I don't appreciate being blindsided. Last time I checked, couples make decisions together." I lay back in the seat, not wanting to speak another word to him for the rest of the way.

As we entered the hotel room, he said, "Listen, Nya—"

"I'm tired, hot, and sweaty, and don't feel like talking. Good night." I went to the bathroom and slammed the door. All I wanted to do was take a hot shower and go to sleep.

Overall, we had such a fun day, I thought. I climbed in the bed hoping I made it clear to Vince to stay his distance away from me. I needed some cool-down time.

"I apologize for not letting you know I wanted you to meet my family. You're so important to me," he whispered in my ear. "I love you and just got so excited about bringing you home to meet them. Due to the demands of the business, I don't have the luxury of visiting them often. I thought this would be great opportunity. I agree with you. We are in this together, and I should have discussed it with you first."

"I forgive you."

"Glad to hear it." Vince hugged me and slid his hands toward my panties. He slid them off.

"What are you doing?"

"I have a date with your clit. She's been waiting for me all day."

Vince opened my legs and slid his tongue into my love cave, giving me no choice but to cum in his mouth.

Chapter 47

Vince gently rubbed my back. "Is everything okay between us?"

"Yes. We had our first fight since becoming official, that's all. I forgive you and want to move forward" I rubbed my nose against his.

For the first few months in a relationship, men tend to be on their best behavior. Then their true colors come out. Vince tended to jump the gun a bit. That was okay, as long as he was able to recognize and correct it. I had issues as well but, what was important was we could work them out.

"So do I. Now, our final destination will be the island of Turks and Caicos. Our flight leaves in about two and a half hours."

"Wow!" I giggled, feeling excited. "I want to get a few more bites of breakfast, and then we can go."

"I should try to eat a little bit myself. We'll be in the air for a while."

"Do you think we can visit Kennesaw more often? I really enjoyed spending time here."

He nodded. "I can definitely arrange that."

Upon arriving on the island, I learned we were staying at the exclusive Windsong Resort. Our oceanfront suite came with a Jacuzzi, rooftop terrace, grill, high-definition television, and cozy lounge chairs. Marble countertops, stainless steel appliances, washer, dryer, and gourmet kitchen were included in the package. An all-day spa and fitness center was an extra bonus during our time at the resort.

We didn't hesitate swimming in the turquoise water and walking on the powdered sands. Each morning I would wake up and sit outside to soak up the air and atmosphere. And, at night, I'd crack the door open to hear the waves, which gave me such a relaxing feeling.

I couldn't get enough of the red ruby grapefruit and the sweet orange served at the continental breakfast every morning.

Every day, I tried something new. Vince enjoyed the pecan-crusted mahimahi with rice and peas I prepared for him. While shopping at a market, a local woman was kind enough to give me the recipe. For my last dinner on the island,

I had a tender, moist piece of lamb with steam vegetables wrapped in a pita.

In the four days we stayed, Vince and I went sailing, horseback riding, diving, kayaking, sailing, and snorkeling. We took countless pictures, and we had the memories to cherish.

After arriving home, for a moment, I didn't want to go back to work. But once I pulled a stack of bills out the mailbox, the reality set in. This month was going to be the first time that I had to pay the mortgage all by myself.

After sorting through the bills and unwanted junk mail, I saw a letter all citizens across the United States of America dread—a court summons for jury duty.

Chapter 48

I tried to fake being pregnant to get out of jury duty. It didn't work. Unless I was going to be hospitalized, reporting to criminal courthouse room number five at the Chesapeake General District Court was a priority. Finding a doctor to sign off on a lie wasn't worth the trouble.

Ten years ago, my aunt couldn't find a substitute teacher for her classes and failed to call the night before to see if she had to appear. She decided to go to work and not leave her high school students stranded for the day. Since she failed to report to jury duty, the system tracked her down and hit her with penalties and fines for not showing up in court. She had to pay a hefty price and serve on the very next case.

Unfortunately, at jury selection, I was hand-picked by the defense team. When the defendant's lawyer looked my way and nodded, I knew I was destined to be a juror on the case.

The trial for Mr. Andrew Keeman began at nine o'clock in the morning. He was on trial for the murder of his wife. On the night of the murder in question, Keeman claimed he came home to hear a screaming match between his wife Heather and another man. The man kept ordering his wife to go upstairs to the master bedroom. Keeman testified that he entered through the back door of the house and quietly went upstairs and waited in their bedroom shower to surprise the perpetrator. He stayed in the shower until he heard a loud gunshot. By the time he came out of the shower, it was too late. The gunman had already shot his wife in the head. Keeman claimed that, as he approached, the gunman shot his wife in the head a second time. He said he tried to wrestle him to the carpet floor and take the gun away from him, but he got shot in the arm, and the culprit ran away.

The bailiff announced, "All rise. Honorable Judge Barry Slotkin."

"I can't hear," Mr. Berry, another juror declared, pointing to his ears.

"Good morning, ladies and gentlemen. I'm James Farrell, the district attorney for the City of Chesapeake. I will prove to you in this courtroom that Andrew Keeman viciously murdered his wife for money. Mrs. Keeman had six life insurance policies on his wife totaling two million dollars. Throughout this case, I will take you into the world of his double life. Ultimately, Andrew Keeman thought he was entitled to the good life. Instead of working hard for the fruits of his labor, killing his wife was an easier plan."

"I can't hear," Mr. Berry announced again. This time, he was standing up.

The judge requested Mr. Farrell repeat his opening statement. Then it was the defense's turn.

"Good morning, folks. My name is Gerald Sebert, the defendant's attorney. It's heartwrenching and sad what happened to the Keeman family. I'm here today to prove to you Andrew Keeman didn't murder his beloved wife of fifteen years and mother of his four children. The evidence will speak for itself and prove this man's innocence," he stated, pointing to the defendant.

"I can't hear," Mr. Berry replied for the third time, tugging on his ears.

"Mr. Berry, we can't continue to have these interruptions. We need to get you proper hearing equipment before we can proceed. Court is adjourned until tomorrow morning at the same time, nine o'clock." The judge hurried off to his chambers.

I wasn't sure I could take another moment of this.

***

The trial went on for two weeks and three days. Since the case was high-profile, with television and radio stations swarming around the courthouse to get the latest buzz, the jurors were sequestered in a nearby hotel to discuss the case. On a few nights, Vince snuck into my room to keep me company.

We were a hung jury until one juror, Missy Swain, pointed out a picture taken in the shower. It showed a can of beer on the shower floor. It was found to be three-fourths full. If your wife was being shot by an intruder, why would you be drinking a beer?

No other DNA was found at the crime scene, except his and his wife's. The most damaging testimony was that of a neighbor who was outside at the time of the murder and didn't see any intruder. All he saw was Mr. Keeman coming home late, which was unusual for him.

Mr. Keeman's wounds appeared to be self-inflicted, and a forensics examination found his fingerprints on the gun used to kill his wife. They also found gunpowder residue on his right hand. He claimed he grabbed the gun to try to shoot the intruder while they were wrestling. According to him, he fired one shot and missed. What didn't add up was, only two bullet shells were found at the crime scene, and there was no trace of a third shot being fired.

With evidence stacked against him, Andrew Keeman was found guilty of first-degree murder, and the jury sought the death penalty. The guilty verdict meant that the four Keeman children were now orphans.

After the verdict was announced Heather's brother jumped the benches when no one was paying attention and wrestled Keeman to the ground. Once he got him on the floor, the brother stomped him on his head repeatedly.

Four bailiffs had to pry the brother away from Keeman. People were screaming and running out of the blood-splattered courtroom. Quickly, more bailiffs showed up on the scene to get control of the matter at hand.

Chapter 49

"Nya, in case you didn't know, medical scrubs isn't the new look for the summer. You should buy yourself some new clothes," Leah informed me while checking online for new dresses.

I was in her bedroom watching *The Game*, a show on the CW television network. "You go through money like it's liquid in your hands, whether your bills are paid or not. Right now, I don't have the luxury of spending what I have. I have other priorities."

"Well, if you change your mind, I'm on my way to Nordstrom's to try on and buy this dress I've been eyeing for weeks. I just got paid and don't have a care in the world."

"I refuse to see you spend cable and light bill money on a dress."

"You're just jealous."

"Yeah, right. Well, you go on without me. I'm sure I won't change my mind about going."

"Will you be here when I get back?"

"No, I'm leaving out too. I'm still putting in overtime hours to make ends meet," I explained, grabbing my things to leave.

"Hey, babe," I said to Vince on my cell phone as I walked to my car.

"Hey, beautiful. What are you up to?"

"I'm just leaving Leah's and am on my way to work. How's the new kid doing on the job site?"

"He's not doing as well as I thought he would. To be honest, I'm disappointed. He talked himself up at the interview, but now he's definitely not delivering on his word. The kid is lazy and always has excuses. Those two things are my pet peeves. If he doesn't get it together, I will have to let him go, plain and simple. I laugh, joke, and try my best to maintain a positive work environment for my guys. All I ask in return is that they do their job."

"I agree. Well, I'm off to the hospital. I can't stay on the phone because I left my headset at home. See you later, Rappaport." I kissed him through the phone before saying good-bye.

I couldn't wait for my shift to be over. I was spending the night at Vince's, and we had a great plans set up for weekend.

The annual Food and Wine Festival was swarming with people at the Norfolk Scope in the arena and Exhibition Hall. Not many were willing to pass up sampling dishes from celebrity chefs like grill guru, Bobby Flay, Paula Deen, and cooking partners Pat and Gina Neely.

Also, this was an advertising haven for new chefs to try out their dishes. Butterfly chicken stuffed with spinach and feta cheese was the big hit. People kept going for second and third helpings.

Since I was in the mood for cheese, I tried a creamy cheese fondue on bite sized fresh baked pretzels. Fruit eaten with pecorino Romano cheese enhanced the flavor.

On the third Saturday of each month in the spring, summer, and fall, Seabring Park in Virginia Beach transformed in a drive-in movie. The movies ranged from black-and-white oldies to movies of 2001.

Tonight's feature was *Love & Basketball*. I always got teary-eyed at the end when the main characters, Quincy and Monica, decide to give their relationship another try. They were destined to be together.

After the movie, the owners of the park didn't like anyone to leave without dancing to a song. Otis Redding's "These Arms of Mine" started playing through the speakers.

Vince extended his hand out to me. "May I have this dance?"

"Yes." I nodded, smiling.

"Nya, you feel so good," he said, holding me close as we slow-danced. What we have is so special. I will always cherish it."

"This feels right."

We had come to the realization that both of our parents had experienced an old-school love affair. Vince and I longed for the same thing. My dream was to be happily married for the rest of my life. Longevity, memories, and building a life together with the one I love were vital to me.

Later on that night, Vince enchanted my G-spot after he caught a glimpse of my purple bra and G-string set.

Chapter 50

Thankfully, I had the day off today. People were paying up to one hundred dollars to exchange shifts. My best pals, my family, along with their family members and friends, were looking forward to the event of a lifetime.

"Let's do a quick check. It's supposed to be cold tonight. Do you have insulated gloves, earmuffs, and a thick scarf?" Vince inquired.

"Yep, I have everything except the earmuffs. Besides, my world-famous cocoa will keep me warm. If all else fails, I'll just stand right next to you, so you can keep me warm."

"Do you want to use one of my hats?"

"Since there's no time to run to Sports Authority, I'll have to settle for yours." I reached out for the hat.

"Beggars can't be choosers."

We started laughing.

Though we arrived at the Obama rally two hours before he was scheduled to speak, thousands of people had already beat us there. While waiting, Vince and I handed out twenty-five dozen Krispy Kreme classic doughnuts. All we asked in return was that everyone share and pass the box down to the next person.

Before Barack Obama made his way to the stage, he shook many hands. Tara's father and I were one of the fortunate ones. When shaking his hand, I felt as though I was touching a piece of history in the making. During these times of uncertainty and crisis, all people could do was cling to their faith, and hope the economy and these heartwrenching times would turn around.

Since Vince had visited his family for Thanksgiving, he decided to spend Christmas with me. After eating a hearty meal at my parents' house and taking extra plates, we went back to his place for an all-night Christmas movie marathon. We watched *National Lampoon's Christmas Vacation*, *This Christmas*, *A Christmas Story*, *Love Actually*, *The Family Stone*, and *A Charlie Brown Christmas*. Munching on kettle corn and sipping on Shirley Temple cocktails with cherries on top made the night even more special.

Chapter 51

"What a day," I whispered to myself while turning the key to enter in the front door. My overnight shift was finally over. We had received four inches of snow last night, and the roads were horrible, but I managed to get home safely by driving as slow as I could. It took me forever to make it. I was petrified of swerving into another lane on the icy roads, so I took my sweet time. Yesterday, I had put salt on the porch and all over in the driveway, so the steps weren't that bad for me to walk on.

"Nya, you finally got home. I've been waiting for you," a voice bombarded me.

The next thing I know, I fell on my knees in disbelief and shock. "Tory!" I screamed.

"Yes, it's me, baby. I'm here now," he declared, picking me up.

"Put me down! What happened to your face?"

"All right, I'll put you down. If you let me explain, I will tell you about the fire."

As I looked into his eyes, it felt as if I was dreaming. While paying close attention, I made sure everything was still intact. No broken bones, or missing teeth, but he had plenty of scars on him. His voice was deep and raspy.

"Tory, you left me without a word of good-bye, just a sorry-ass note. I looked for you, but never turned up anything. I wasted thousands of dollars trying to find you for months."

"I know you were probably looking for me, but I had to kick the booze on my own. I almost lost my life because of it. If it wasn't for the fire, I wouldn't be here today."

With every breath I took, repressed anger and rage started building up. "How could you do that to me? I loved you!" I screamed again, pushing him away.

"I'm sorry," he said, inching closer to me. "I know I have plenty of explaining to do."

I kept pushing him away, and the pushing quickly turned into hits.

"You don't give a crap about me, your family, or our marriage. My birthday, Thanksgiving, and Christmas went by without one word from you. I thought you were dead. In the back of my mind, I thought a police officer would come to my door saying they found you dead in a back alleyway. I've worried sick over you. When you left me, I was left with the burden of dealing with a stress-induced peptic ulcer. Thank you so much. What a heartless and selfish husband you are! Your poor mother hasn't been the same since you left. Tory, you think you can do whatever the hell you want and get away with it. I hate you!" I shouted while hitting him.

Tory used his hands to block my hits. When I finally calmed down, he lifted me up and carried me into the living room.

"I'm sorry," he kept repeating as he held me close.

He made the mistake of kissing me, and I bit his bottom lip. "Let go of me." I pushed him away from me.

"No." He refused to let go of me still holding me close and attempted to kiss me again.

My emotions finally took over, and I kissed him back. I hadn't realized how much I really missed him. The touch of his skin was what I'd been yearning for.

Tory gently laid me on the living room floor. While we were kissing, he took off the pants of my scrubs. Then, after he took off his jeans, he slid his python in the place he knew so well, and my pussy welcomed him.

"I hurt you. I'm sorry. Please forgive me," he expressed, gazing into my eyes as he thrust his dick in and out of me.

His strokes felt so good. "You hurt me so deep by abandoning our marriage," I cried out.

Tory started kissing me again. "I won't ever leave you again," he said in my ear.

"Liar!" I blurted out, crying.

"Shhh," he cooed, caressing my hair.

I felt myself about to climax. I tried hard to fight it but to no avail. Only Tory could make my whole body shake uncontrollably. When Tory came, he held me tight as we both lay there.

Once I had the strength to stand up, I sat on the couch to put my pants back on. "Get out!" I hollered at the top of my lungs, confused about what had just happened.

"This is my home. I'm not leaving." He rose to his feet.

"No, you're sadly mistaken. This is my damn house. You don't live here anymore, loser," I informed him as he put his clothes back on. I literally shoved him out of the house.

"Nya, please don't shut me out of your heart!"

"No! When you had my heart, you didn't know what to do with it. Don't try to set foot in this home. I'm changing the security code, and I'm removing your name from the Brink's security system. We're over. Go back to wherever you came from." I slammed the door in his face.

My head spinning, I accidentally walked into the table in the foyer, and the cordless phone fell to the floor. I called the only person I felt could help me with this situation.

Steven answered the phone. "Hello?"

"Steven, it's Nya. Come get your brother. He's standing on my porch, and I want him to leave now!" I yelled out.

Chapter 52

"What!"

I heard the phone drop. "Hello! Hello!" I called out.

"Nya, I'm still here. Sorry, I accidentally dropped the phone. Where did he come from? Where the hell has he been all this time?"

"I don't know. Right now, I don't care. Please come get him." I hung up the phone.

While Tory was steadily banging on the front door, I ran upstairs to the spare bedroom to get the rest of his belongings. Funny, I had been contemplating giving his clothes to Goodwill.

"Here are the rest of your clothes," I declared while dumping five storage bins on the lawn.

Just then, Steven pulled up in the driveway and was trying to take Tory with him.

"Nya, please . . . Can I just have thirty minutes to explain?"

"No! By the way, I want a divorce!" I shouted and slammed the door once again.

***

Rage and bitterness still consumed me the next morning. I thought I would cry and become a walking zombie just like when he'd first left. Today, I didn't shed one damn tear.

I switched shifts with some coworkers, so I could have the next few days off to get my head straight. When I wasn't right emotionally, I tended to make mistakes. When dealing with people's lives, mistakes should be kept to a minimum, so I wasn't about to take any chances.

All I really wanted to do was punch Tory in the face. How could he think he could just come back, simply explain what happened, and then everything would be okay? To top it off, we had sex without a condom. I was fertile as hell.

I quickly ran into the bathroom to see if I had the morning-after pill. The last thing I needed was to be pregnant by him. He turned out to be a horrible husband and most likely wouldn't do well as a father. I spotted the pills in the medicine cabinet. "Thank God!" I declared at the top of my lungs.

In the afternoon, I spoke with the lawyer to confirm serving divorce papers to Tory. Since we didn't have any children, we had to be legally separated for only six months for everything to go through.

Many thoughts were swarming in my head. *Would Tory even sign the papers? Would I have to sell the house?* To be honest, I loved this house and didn't want to leave. *Could I continue to afford to pay the mortgage, homeowner association dues, and utilities all by myself? What about Vince?*

"I can't wait to see you," Vince said, after picking up his phone.

I hadn't spoken to him since I'd left the hospital yesterday morning, so he had no idea what had happened since then.

"Hey. How's your day so far?"

"It's cool. So far I'm having a typical busy day. Two checks from prominent business owners bounced on me. With winter rearing its ugly head, people are calling to get their heating systems repaired or want new ones installed. How's your day going? You getting ready for work?"

"It's going fine. I switched shifts with a co-worker so I could have the day off. I'm not really feeling well today, so I'm just going to stay home. Can I see you later on in the week?" I asked, wanting some time alone.

"Sure, it's no problem. I miss you though. Besides, the weatherman is already saying the roads will be icy tomorrow morning. I want you to be safe."

"I miss you too. I'll give you a ring later on."

No Tory in sight today, I thought. I sent a text blast to Tara, Yvette, and Leah, informing them that Tory had come back.

Just then, Tory showed up again, and was pacing back and forth on the front porch. I sent the girls another message that he was outside my house. I didn't know why he came back. Maybe, he was hoping I would open the door.

Within forty minutes, Tara, Yvette and Leah were standing outside my front door.

"Why would you hurt my sister like that?" Leah demanded to know, throwing snowballs at him.

Soon after, Tara joined in. "Tory, you're fucked up!"

Yvette had to convince the both of them to come in the house. "Y'all, it's too cold out here. Let's go in the house."

"I can't believe he had the nerve to come back," Yvette announced after closing the front door.

"Turn the heat up," Leah said.

"I've got it on seventy-three degrees."

"It's not enough. Turn it up to seventy-five, so it can be warm and toasty in here. With you, being wrapped in the Snuggie fleece blankets every chance you get, it's hard for you to feel the nip in the air."

"Yes, I do love my Snuggie."

"I'm going to boil water for some tea," Yvette said, and we all followed her into the kitchen.

Tara pulled out orange-flavored green tea and biscotti cookies dipped in chocolate from the pantry. "So when did the jerk get here?"

"Yesterday."

"Why didn't you call us earlier?"

"You all have lives, Yvette. Besides, it was late, around eleven, and on a school night."

"What did he have to say for himself?" Leah asked.

"I never gave him the opportunity to really say anything. I don't want to hear any more lies or excuses. For all I know, he could very well still be an alcoholic. I don't want to know. I don't want to have to deal with it. Right when I'm really trying to move on with on my life, his behind shows up. I had to take the ringer off the house phone. Tory called at least every fifteen minutes. On my cell phone, the ritual became every half an hour. Today after he leaves, I plan to put my car in the garage, so he won't think I'm here. He'll leave eventually. I doubt he'll stay out there all day."

Yvette shrugged her shoulders. "Maybe he did seek treatment." She took out coffee mugs from the cabinet.

"At this point, does it really matter?" Leah bit into a cookie. "It's a little too late to be coming back."

"Only Nya can decide if it matters or not," Yvette replied, pouring the hot water into the mugs and settling tea bags in them.

"I despise him. I'm so pissed. I thought this anger had disappeared, until I saw him again yesterday."

"Did you tell Vince yet?" Tara asked.

"No, I was supposed to see him tonight, but canceled. I'll tell him when I'm ready though."

"I'm hungry," Leah blurted out.

"There's leftover spaghetti in the refrigerator. Heat it all up in the microwave, so everyone can get a plate."

"Wait. I hear a car pulling up." Leah ran to look out the window. "Tory is getting in the car with his brother."

"I didn't think he would stay here all day," I responded.

"Overall, are you all right? You can stay with Jarvis, the kids, and me if you need to get away."

"No, I'll be fine. I'm stronger than I thought I was. Really, I just want him to leave me alone."

"Do you truly want a divorce?" Tara questioned.

"Yes, I think so. It's for the best. I'll have less drama in my life. I refuse to take him back. I don't want to be put through what he did to me ever again. If I get back with him, I'll be taking that risk."

A week went by with no Tory in sight. I'd been going over to Vince's house. I didn't know what would've happened if Vince came to the house and Tory showed up.

The temperature had risen and melted most of the snow away. Kids in my neighborhoods were disappointed to see their masterpiece snowmen dwindling down to water.

"Are you all right?" Vince asked while we were watching the show, *Ghost Whisperer*.

"Yeah, I'm fine. Overtime hours are getting to me, that's all."

"Now that you mentioned it, you have been working a lot of overtime hours. Why?"

"Well, I switched a couple of shifts to get a few days off last week, and I had already signed up for extra hours. I need the extra money. I've been paying all the bills by myself. Car payments, mortgage, and utilities all add up. I have to admit, I'm proud of myself for not charging anything on the credit cards to make ends meet."

"I don't mind helping you. How much do you need?"

"Listen, I appreciate your help, but I'm managing it on my own. Those sausages Stromboli are probably ready in the oven. I brought extra tomato sauce, just the way you like it." I grabbed his arm and led the way into the kitchen.

Chapter 53

"Good morning." Tory beamed as I locked the front door.

"The security system is on. Go in at your own risk."

"I got my old job back with Irv. He was happy to see me. I started last Wednesday. The team welcomed me back. It felt good to be back."

I completely ignored him and got in my car to go to work. After a week of him not showing up, I was sure he wasn't coming back again. I couldn't help but wonder how long he was going to keep this up.

"Happy Friday." Tory smiled. He had a blueberry muffin in his hand from Starbucks. He knew it was one of my favorites in the morning.

All I did was look at him.

"Umm, I have a copy of the program I completed. Please, Nya, just look at it. Plus, I have the name and number of the director of the facility because, knowing how you are, you would call and verify. Hell, you may even want to go to see if the place is legit and standing." He chuckled.

I didn't see anything funny. "Off to work," I replied.

Every morning, Tory would stop by the house to greet me before he went to work. Every evening, after he got off work, he would sit on the porch on a lawn chair till one in the morning, hoping I would talk to him.

Forty-six days later, Tory hadn't missed one day of the routine. Plus, he would leave cards on my car windshield.

Leah, Yvette, and Tara were beginning to let up on him and had the nerve one day to offer him leftover meatloaf, mashed potatoes, peas, and a glass of fresh-made tea. He apologized to them and thanked them for being there for me. With him being in a fire, they showed even more mercy on him. Before long, I began to look forward to seeing him in the morning and the evening.

Matter of fact, he even got the nerve to go to my parents' house to talk to them about what happened. He sat there with Mommy and Daddy pleading his case and apologized to them. Mommy said pray about it. Daddy said he would stand by me with whatever decision I made, but to keep in mind that "a man's actions means more than his words." He said he didn't want to see me hurt anymore, and that all he cared about was my happiness.

Today, I got off early, so the plumber could repair the kitchen sink, which had a major clog. I decided to put the trash can down the driveway for pickup tomorrow morning.

"Good afternoon," Ms. Susie, my neighbor across the street, addressed me.

Ms. Susie's husband had died of a stroke a few years back. Now she clung to her cat Riley for comfort. Oftentimes, I'd see her walking Riley through the neighborhood in a sealed-up stroller.

"Hi, Ms. Susie. How are you?"

"Doll, I'm fine. It's you I'm worried about."

"Why is that?"

"Well, it doesn't take a genius to figure Tory and you have been dealing with marital problems. He comes here every morning and night just to talk to you. I think it's so sweet. When I used to get mad at Harold, I wish he'd done the same for me. Whatever he did, I forgave him. I don't know all the details of your situation, but I hope it has a happy ending just like the Lifetime movies. I've got to run. It was nice talking to you." She got in her car and drove off.

Soon after, Steven dropped Tory off for the normal routine.

"Hi, I visited Mom today," Tory said, walking up the driveway.

"Hello. How's Mrs. Sothers doing?"

"She's doing fine, trying to feed me anything in the house. The last thing I want is for her to worry about me, especially since I've been in a fire."

"I'm glad to hear she's doing well," I said, ignoring his last statement.

"Nya, I hope you've been reading the cards I leave for you and not throwing them away. I got paid, and Irv gave me some extra money to catch up on bills. Here is the money for the mortgage and car payments for the next two months. I'm sorry if you've been struggling lately. I went to the restaurant and saw Rome on my lunch break. He and you have done a fantastic job with the place. I plan to start managing the restaurant in a few months. I got the divorce papers you had delivered at Steven's house. I guess you figured I've been laying my head there. You're right. He's been letting me stay with him since he sees I'm trying to get my life back together."

"Thank you." I took the envelope from him, trying hard not to smile. It felt good to hear that he acknowledged everything I'd been doing by myself, holding down the fort since he'd vanished into thin air.

"So you know, I'm not ready to sign the papers. I'm still going to fight for us, Nya. Every day is a new day. Each day, I hope you will talk to me more. Maybe one day you'll let me back into your heart. It's ultimately where I belong."

"I don't care what you want. I didn't want you to leave me, and you did. Besides, I've been seeing someone else," I said back to him, being spiteful.

"Are you in love with him? What's his name?"

"What am I going to tell you his name for? So you can track him down and confront him? Why? For every cause, there is an effect. I painfully realized you didn't give a shit about me, so I moved on with my life. Deal with it."

"Nya, I need to know if you're in love with him. If you are, no matter what I do, it won't matter anymore. Please tell me if I've lost you for good."

"Since you want to pay for it, Tory, you can have the truck. I'll have it in the driveway ready for you tomorrow morning. Bye." I slammed the door in his face.

Chapter 54

"What's happening?"

"Ma'am, my name is Nya. You're in the hospital. A nice man found you wandering in the park. He saw a bruise on your head, and you told him you had accidentally bumped into a tree and fallen down," I informed her.

"Do you know what your name is?" I asked the woman, who appeared to be in her late sixties.

"No," she responded, shaking her head.

"Do you know your phone number or the name of a relative who we can contact?"

"I don't know. I'm so confused."

"Well, lie back. I'm going to take your vital signs and blood for normal procedure. You've got a mild concussion."

After two hours of gently probing Jane Doe, her daughter, granddaughter, and husband came into the emergency room on a whim. This hospital was the first one on the list. Her name was Millie Babcock. I wasn't surprised when the family confided in me that she suffered from Alzheimer's disease.

"Dad, we've got to put her in a home," the daughter pleaded. "It's for her safety."

"I can't leave her. Besides, your mother can wander off in a home too. It's my fault. I fell asleep because I haven't got any rest in days."

"You haven't got any rest because you've been watching over Mamma like a hawk," she replied.

"I'll do better. We'll hire nurses to come to the house and tend to her. I love her so much. We've been together for fifty-one years," he said, holding on tight to his wife's hand.

In that moment, the only person I truly wanted to grow old with was Tory. For a while, I'd been wrestling with my feelings, which had been keeping me up at night. The truth and reality was, I was still in love with Tory. It hurt me to know he endured being in a fire and I wasn't there for him. If he ended up a cripple or barely recognizable, I would've still loved him. Always. I knew what I had to do.

I had gone to Vince's office and waited for all his employees, including Nancy, his nosy assistant, to leave before I barged in. "He came back," I announced.

Vince suddenly stopped looking at the invoices on his desk and looked up at me. "Tory came back?"

I nodded, tears in my eyes. "Yes."

"How long has he been here?"

"He's been here for a while."

"Has he been staying with you?"

"No. His brother's house."

"Where does that leave us? Please, Nya, don't give me any bullshit."

"The reality is, we got together on the pretense he wouldn't come back, but he did. I've come to the realization that, even after all this time, I'm still in love with him. Plus, I don't want to be with you, knowing in the back of my head that I'll always be wondering what could have been if I had given him another chance."

"Nya, you gave him a chance, and he bailed out on you and his rehab program."

"So did your mother. Many times. Now look at her. She recovered. Your parents are the spitting image of happiness. Vince, it may not hold a lot of weight with you, but I'm truly sorry for hurting you. I decided to go with my heart and not my head," I said, gently rubbing his face.

"I feel as though someone has thrown a brick at my heart. At least you were honest with me from the beginning. I thank you for that. I'm going to miss you. He better make you happy. That man doesn't know how fortunate he is." Vince gave me a kiss and a hug.

"You are a wonderful man, and I wish nothing but the best for you."

As I tried to walk out the door, Vince blurted out, "Nya, did you sleep with him before breaking up with me?"

"Vince, don't ask questions you really don't want to know the answer to," I said and blew him a kiss.

Chapter 55

During my lunch break, I contemplated whether I'd just made an enormous mistake choosing Tory over Vince. *Only time will tell, I guess.* While waiting in my car for Tory to pull up in the driveway, I popped in Corinne Bailey Rae's CD and tried to relax.

Just then Steven pulled up to drop Tory off. I almost hit him with the car door when I opened it.

"You got here before me," Tory said, his briefcase in one hand and the infamous lawn chair in the other.

"You want to talk. Here's your chance." I led the way into the house.

"The house still smells the same," he said after entering into the foyer. "It's Seaside Breeze by Renuzit."

"If you want something to eat or drink, before we talk, get it yourself."

"No, I'm ready to talk right now. Believe me, I'm more ready to explode because I've been dying to explain to you what happened."

"You have the floor. Speak." I nodded while he sat down in the love seat, and I parked myself on the couch.

"Well, do you remember my college buddy Todd who came to visit a few times?"

"Yeah."

"He majored in psychology and runs a clinic in Dallas, Texas. The day before I left, he happened to call to check on me after he'd heard from Kevin that my father had passed away and I wasn't doing too well. I poured my feelings out to him, and he suggested that I fly out there and enter into his program. I passed. Here is the certificate." He retrieved a piece of paper from his briefcase and handed it to me.

After talking with Steven, who gave me the name of the facility, I had called to verify that the facility was real. Yes, Tory did know me well. "It seems Wake Forest has helped you."

"Yes, it has helped me a lot. I first had to realize that I had to be willing to help myself."

"What happened with the fire? How did that come about?"

"Late one night, I snuck out of the facility to meet up with a guy that had been kicked out of the program. We were at his house and after chugging down three bottles of whisky, vodka, and rum, we were all out of liquor. He went to the store to get some more. I was hungry and went into his kitchen to heat up a chicken and cheese Hot Pockets. Not paying attention, I turned the oven to four hundred and fifty degrees. I passed out on the kitchen floor.

"The next thing I know, I was in the hospital for burns and smoke inhalation. This is the reason why you see all these scars on my body. I know I may not look exactly the same, but I'm still the Tory you fell in love with."

He took off his suit to show me his scars, which I hadn't noticed the day we had sex.

"Looks don't have anything to do with this. I'm not a superficial person. Don't try to use your major fuckup as a way to get people to feel sorry for you."

"I'm not." He shook his head as he put his clothes back on.

"You were so lucky to survive the fire."

"Yes, I was. Besides aching pain and going through many skin graft procedures, I'm all right. What I've learned through all of this is that I'm truly meant to be here. More importantly, the hospital paid for all of my medical bills, courtesy of Todd. His uncle happens to be on the committee board for the hospital."

"What did the rehab center teach you?" I asked, poking his brain.

"It taught me the twelve-step program. At first, I spent months sneaking in alcohol and trying to get other patients to join in my misery. Todd wanted to kick my ass and laid it out plain and simple, saying I had a choice of life or death. He was ready to kick me out of the program. Todd lost his father too, five years ago, so we really connected, as far as our feelings. He went through the same thing as me. I know Pop isn't coming back. It hurts like hell, but I don't want to drink myself to death anymore or hurt those who love and care about me."

"Why didn't you bother to call me, Steven, Anne, your mother, or anyone to let us know you were still alive?"

"At first, I didn't call because I was too wrapped up into getting my lips around an alcohol bottle. I would have just pushed you away even more. Then, I didn't want any of you to see me at my lowest point in the hospital. Finally, I had enough of the booze and made a personal stand to focus all my energy into getting better. When I thought about how I hurt you, my mother, and my siblings, it motivated me even more to kick my habit. Not having any contact with anyone was the most effective solution. It's the reason why I left my wallet with debit and credit cards and cell phone here . . . I knew you would come looking for me. The only thing I did take was my driver's license."

"What do you want now?"

"I want to come back home and have us start all over again. I don't want to go back to the way it was before my father died. I know it will never be the same. I just want our love and our relationship to grow stronger. All I know is, I want to do the right thing and live my life. I take it day by day. It's not going to be easy, but I want you by my side." Tory kissed my hand and looked to me for approval to rebuild our relationship.

"I love you too. If I see or even think you've had a drink, it's over. I can't take living my life in misery. I'm proud of you that you got help. Steven and Rome have been making it a point to text me about your progress at work and the restaurant. I agree, let's take it day by day and concentrate on rebuilding our marriage. I'll be right back." I ran to the bedroom. I went to my dresser and drawer and found exactly what I was looking for. I ran back into the living room. "Now put the wedding ring back on my hand." I handed him my ring with a big smile on my face.

After he put it on my finger, I asked him, "Where's your wedding ring?"

"In Texas. I pawned it for liquor." Tory lowered his head.

"It's all right. Thank goodness, I have insurance on it."

He grinned. "You're always a step ahead."

"True. Are you hungry?"

"A little."

"While you stop by Steven's house to get your clothes and shoes, I'll make fajitas. Which would you prefer, steak or chicken?"

"Can we have both?"

"Sure." I nodded and hugged him.

"I'm glad you chose me. I promise not to hurt you ever again."

Later on that day, while listening to Stevie Wonder, I helped Tory put his belongings back into our closet. Even though, I was uncertain about the future, I felt as though I'd made the right decision.

Chapter 56

Two months had gone by, and so far, so good. Mommy suggested we have a party with our friends and family to celebrate, but I declined. I was too concerned with Tory and me focusing on having a normal life.

Tara, Rob, Nelson, Leah, Jarvis, and Yvette all welcomed him back with open arms. It took a while, but Daddy accepted him back into the family. Last Sunday, when we went over for dinner, Daddy made it a point to shake and squeeze Tory's hand extra firm.

"Next Thursday, will you be able to make it home by four o'clock? The Terminix Company is coming out to do a preventive treatment for termites and other bugs. Since the commercial kept coming on, I thought it would be a good idea to get it done. Plus, you know I wouldn't be able to sleep at night with bugs flying around here. I tried to get time off, but three nurses will be out that day."

Tory continued rubbing my feet. He nodded. "Yeah, I can."

"Hmm. Why do you have so many cuts and scars around your face?"

"Aah. One of my many self-inflicted accidents at the rehab place. It had a strict curfew policy. One night, while sneaking out to grab a bottle of Bacardi rum, I hopped out of the window from the second floor and landed on my face. I ended up needing ten stitches."

"Oh, I bet that hurt. Any other mishaps you need to tell me about?"

"Nope."

"You were definitely a bad boy. If it wasn't for your friendship, Todd would have kicked you out of the program."

"That's correct. Have you thought about leaving this area and relocating to Charlotte, North Carolina?"

"No, we've talked about it before and agreed we would stay here."

"I know, but I'm talking about retiring there. Oh well, it's just a thought." He let my feet go and placed a gentle peck on my lips. "Let me rub you down."

"All right."

Tory sat me in the bed and took off my T-shirt and panties. "Your body is still as beautiful as the first time we made love."

"The first time was so romantic and exciting."
I giggled.

"Yeah. Remember we were on the beach? The
moon was looking down on us. I chased you in
the house—"

"No, we went to the beach on our first date,"
I corrected him. "The first time, we had sex, you
snagged a room at the Odyssey Hotel filled with
rose petals, fruit, and romantic music. I will
never forget that night."

"Yes, I remember now," he stated, rubbing
down my shoulders.

"Hmm! It feels good what you're doing to me."

"How's your shoulder? Does it still hurt?"

I had banged it on the front door the other
morning when I was rushing to leave for work.
"It's good as new."

"I stopped by the bank today to make a deposit
in your account for the bills. I put a little extra in,
just in case you wanted to treat yourself."

"Thank you. I've wanted a fragrance called
Chloe."

"You're welcome. The girls you used to work
with are still talking about the day when you
got shot and the bank was robbed. They even
praised a guy named Darren Edmonds for taking
down the gunman. Why didn't you ever tell me
about him?" Tory was now rubbing my hips, all
the way down toward my ankles.

"He really wasn't worth mentioning. It was due to bad memories, to sum it all up. Remember when we broke up for a while after coming back from Hawaii?

"Yes."

"Well, I dated him for a few months. He turned out to be a bad guy and was just using me to move drugs for him. In the end, Darren ended up dead. He left behind a wife and child, and another woman on the side, which he never bothered to mention to me. Now that I look back, he would have killed me if I got in the way of his power and money." I made sure to leave out the part about the baby. The last thing I wanted was for him to be worried about a past relationship of mine.

"Darren was dead wrong to treat you that way. Did you ever love him?" he asked.

"No, I just got caught up in his charm and relentless pursuit of me."

"Nya, you do love giving a chase."

"Yes, you're right about. With all the lies and deceit, if he didn't die so abruptly, I probably would have broken it off with him anyway. Whether or not, you came back from California wouldn't have made a difference in that decision."

Tory turned me over. "Maybe it was meant to be that he and I never crossed paths. He might have been dead much sooner." He climbed on top of me and began massaging my breasts and then my nipples. He bit the top of my breast.

"Ouch!" I slugged him in the arm.

"Sorry." Tory gently started sucking on my nipples.

Since the night, I let him come back home, I'd decided to wait to have sex again, because I wasn't ready. *Tonight, he might just get lucky.*

Tory turned me over and licked the back of my neck, one of my hot spots. He opened my legs gently and entered my tight pussy.

Tory was relentless, his rather extensive strokes showing me no mercy. Damn, it felt good. It was just what I needed.

"Make me cum," I demanded.

"I won't step till you cum, twice."

"Hmm! Yes, double take, baby!" I shouted.

Later on into the night, Tory was talking in his sleep.

"Nya, I love you, I'll make this up to you. They're all lies they told you," he said in a low tone, with a hint of a Caribbean accent.

I explored his body when he slept, since it bothered him when I looked at it for a while. To be honest, it wasn't as bad as he thought. Plus,

I thought the scars would eventually clear up if he started using those olive oil products a local dermatologist had recommended to me.

Chapter 57

Natalie and Michael sung in unison, "Juice, juice, juice," creating an echo in my ear.

"Would you like grape or apple juice?"

"Apple!" Natalie shouted, jumping in the air.

"Grape!" Michael blurted out with a snotty nose.

I quickly grabbed a tissue from the box. "Let me wipe your nose."

"Auntie Nya, can I watch the *Jon and Kate Plus Eight* show?" Natalie asked. "Hannah is my favorite out of all the kids."

"No, I watch *Little Bill*," Michael whined after I wiped his nose down.

"All right, Michael, while I cook breakfast, you can watch *Little Bill* in the kitchen with me. Natalie, you can watch your show in the living room."

"Okay. What's for breakfast?" Natalie giggled, plopping down on the couch.

"French toast and scrambled eggs."

The kids yelled, "Yeah!"

Since Jarvis was having corrective surgery on his eyes, Tory and I took the kids for the day. He was happy to spend time with them. He played tea party with Natalie and wrestled with Michael all over the house but I think they all enjoyed playing hide-and-seek the most.

Throughout the day, Tory kept hinting to me about having a baby. When he finally had the balls to ask me directly, I was going to tell him I wasn't ready just yet.

It'd been months since he and I decided to give our marriage a try. I was still paranoid and searched the house for alcohol bottles, but every time, I came up empty. We were bonding, getting close again. On Wednesday nights, he watched the National Geographic specials with me, something he never used to do.

I'd noticed some differences in him. He used to prefer his steak medium. Now, he liked it rare. Before all this happened, Tory couldn't live without his Visa check card. Nowadays, the only thing he carried in his wallet was cash and his driver's license. He used to take showers first thing in the morning, but now he waited until around eleven at night to shower, claiming the late shower was his refuge from the day's stress.

I found it strange that he and Rome had been toying with the idea of opening up an upscale Jamaican restaurant. Previously, Tory never really enjoyed Jamaican or island food.

To top everything off, what he did last week was really out of character for him. Since we'd got married, Tory wouldn't dare look at another woman in my presence. Last week, while at a jazz club, he was a bit flirtatious with the waitress, and I caught him checking her out. I wasn't mad about it. I knew it was innocent fun, but he'd never done that before.

After breakfast, the four of us prepared for our day out. Not wanting the kids to fill up on sugars just yet, I gave them plenty of water to drink, whole wheat turkey sandwiches, and seedless grapes for lunch.

"I'm so excited," Natalie expressed. She was holding my hand, while Tory held on to Michael's hand.

"So am I," I admitted as we entered the tent of the UniverSoul Circus.

After buying popcorn, rainbow-colored snow cones, blueberry cotton candy, and memorabilia toys, we marched up the bleachers to watch the show. The horse riders and stiltwalkers performed death-defying acts.

When the tigers came out to perform, the kids were scared. The elephants stole the show by standing up and roaring at the crowd. When the kids became restless, Tory and I knew it was time to go.

"I have to go to the bathroom," Natalie told me.

"All right, let's go. Tory, I'll be right back," I replied.

On the way to the bathroom, I spotted Charles smirking at me from the corner of my eye. I pretended like I hadn't seen him and went straight into the bathroom.

Thankfully, there wasn't a long line to use the bathroom. After we came out the bathroom, I heard a loud commotion in the corner. I tried looking for Tory and Michael, but they were nowhere in sight. Finally, I peeked my head through the crowd and saw Tory choking Charles, his feet lifted off the ground and dangling in the air, and his tongue dangling out of his mouth.

"Tory, what are you doing?" I shouted.

"He was looking at your ass. I don't tolerate disrespect. You got that?"

"Let him go."

"I sure will. It will be my pleasure." Tory dropped him to the floor.

On the way home, we took the kids back to their house, both of them worn out from the day's events.

"What the hell were you thinking, choking him in front of Michael?" I asked after we got home and I had set the alarm system to night mode.

"Nya, I was tired of him looking at you."

"So what if he was looking at me? It doesn't give you the right to choke him. You almost knocked him out. Did you bother to notice his eyes were rolling back into his head? You could have been arrested over that nonsense. Plus, you're teaching the kids to solve their problems physically. Yvette would freak out if she knew what happened."

Tory had a worried look on his face. "Do you think Michael would say something to them?"

"It's not a matter of if he would say something, it's a matter of *when* he will say something. He will probably want to brag on you."

"I apologize. I lost my temper. The last thing I want is to be a negative influence on those kids," he said, shaking his head.

"It's all right. In the morning, I'll call Yvette to smooth things out with her."

I took off my clothes, revealing a lime green bra and boy short set.

"Are you wearing the fragrance Chloe?"

"Courtesy of you," I said, rubbing his hard dick.

Tory motioned me down to the carpet floor. With silk scarves, he tied my hands to the bottom of the bed frame. Then he ripped my panties off and started teasing my pussy, placing the tip of his dick in and out. This kinky game made me want it even more.

Finally, he glided his python inside me for the grand finale.

After fondling each other in the hot shower and reminiscing over fond memories together, we lay in the bed and watched a movie called *G*.

I wasn't tired, but I could tell Tory was fighting sleep. "I love you," I cooed in his ears.

"I love you too, Jewels," he whispered and dozed off to sleep.

Suddenly, I felt as if someone was sitting on my chest. The only person in the world who called me Jewels was Darren Edmonds. *He's supposed to be dead*, I thought as I drifted off to sleep.

Chapter 58

"My back is killing me," Tory moaned.

"It's no wonder. You were doing me for two hours on the floor. You probably threw your back out."

"I'm getting old."

"I have medicine to relieve your pain." I rose up from the bed to get him something to take. I filled a disposable cup with water and handed him the pill and cup.

"Nya, you always know what to do."

"Open your mouth and take this. It will make you feel better."

Tory didn't even bother asking me what pill I'd just popped in his mouth. After twenty minutes, the Percocet kicked in. He didn't feel a thing when I snagged a minor sample of blood from him.

The last time I had seen Darren was on college graduation night when I wore my pink Chanel dress. I took a small strand from the dress to compare DNA samples. I planned to drop these samples off to the lab first thing in the morning.

***

"Feeling better?" I asked, placing his eggs, turkey bacon, and toast on a plate.

"Yes, I am. The pill you gave me helped. What was it?" Tory bit into a slice of bacon.

"It was Aleve I had in the medicine cabinet," I responded, lying through my teeth. I'd made sure to throw the medicine bottle in the trash.

"I hate to eat and run, but Irv is counting on me to nail this new client. I should be home by the usual time. Tonight, you can let your Betty Crocker apron rest, because I'm cooking dinner."

"Surprise me with something tasty." I grinned and kissed him on the cheek good-bye.

I ransacked the house for anything out of the ordinary, like an extra cell phone or loose papers lying around. I patiently waited one hour to call Tory at his office to ensure he was there. Next, my computer geek on call, Aaron, came by to see if the house phone and cell phone were tapped. Plus, I wanted him to make sure no hidden cameras were lurking in the corners. Turning up nothing, I headed off to work.

"Eileen, may I have a rush on these samples? Please make sure the report includes the specific blood type," I said, placing her favorite candy bar, a Butterfinger, on the counter.

"Anything for you."

Digging deeper for more solid information, I dialed the number for Wake Forest Center in Dallas, Texas from an unlisted hospital number. From now on, until I figured out what the hell was going on, I needed to be careful.

"Good morning, Wake Forest Center. This is Mildred speaking. How may I help you?"

"Good morning, Mildred," I said in a Southern drawl, disguising my real voice. "My name is Carolyn, and I would like to enroll my son into the program. He's a cocaine addict and I want to get him some help. I hear Dr. Todd Greene happens to be the best and has helped thousands kick their addiction."

"Oh, dear. I guess you didn't hear."

"Hear what?"

"Honey, I'm sorry to tell you this, but about a year ago, Dr. Todd Greene was brutally murdered. His office was lit on fire. For a month, we had to relocate the patients. The patients took it the worst, especially Tory. He and Todd went to school together. Once the center reopened, Tory and another patient named Raymond didn't return."

That name sounds familiar, I thought. "Did you find out who committed such a heinous crime?"

"No, but it's still an ongoing investigation. The funny thing is, the person who killed Dr. Greene only stole his plaques and a lot of blank certificates. After completing the program, a patient is honored with those items, you know. Honey, I got to run. Right now, the center is packed to capacity. Call me back in about two months, and I'll see if I can spare a bed for your son."

"I sure will. Thank you for your time."

A week later, I'd been researching the medical records of Tory and Darren. Tory's blood type was O negative and healthy as a horse. Darren's blood type was AB positive. He was allergic to morphine, had high blood pressure, an irregular heartbeat, and degenerative disc disease, which caused him severe back pain. Both had similar body builds, but Darren looked younger than his real age.

I was back at Eileen's desk, looking for the test results.

"Here's the report." She handed it over to me.

"Thanks," I replied, taking a deep breath.

"The DNA from the cloth strand and the blood sample were a match. The confirmed blood type is AB positive. I ran it twice to make sure."

Darren's blood type is AB positive, I thought as my knees began to weaken.

Tory was really the presumed dead Darren Edmonds disguising himself. The question was, Why? If the man sleeping in my bed was Darren, where was the real Tory? Was he dead?

Suddenly, I felt I couldn't breathe and went into the closest women's bathroom to collect my thoughts. I felt so alone. *Who could I tell? No one would believe me. Darren posing as Tory could have me committed,* I thought, catching my breath. There was no point in shedding tears.

One thing was for sure, Tory did go to Texas for rehab treatment, and so did Darren. That had to explain why he knew so many things that only Tory and I shared together. One man had died. How many more had been sacrificed due to a psychopath?

"Karen, can you take over my patients? I don't feel so well."

"Sure, I can. What's wrong? You look pale."

"I think I'm coming down with something. I'm going home to rest." I headed to my office to grab my purse.

Quickly, I rushed into the Target store to buy a TracFone. I quickly dialed the phone number of an old friend, Brennon Gilles.

"Hello?"

"Brennon, it's me, Nya."

"Hey. Why are calling me from an unknown number?"

"I'm taking extra precautions. Listen, I need your help right now. To make a long story short, Tory lost his father a few years ago."

"Oh, I'm sorry to hear about that."

"Due to his loss, he became an alcoholic. A year ago, he vanishes into thin air, saying that he went to—"

"He went to Texas," he said, cutting me off.

"What?" I asked in shock.

"Tory went to Texas."

"Did you already know?"

"Yes. Darren was there too. At the time, I didn't put the two clues together. Darren has probably been watching you and him for a long time. With him making a move in Virginia, it wouldn't have been smart for him to do anything else, so he waited till Tory was vulnerable and in Texas. "

"I ran the DNA from a dress Darren gave me. It has his prints all over it. Then I compared it against a blood sample I recently took. Darren is really posing as Tory. He has scars all over his body, claiming he's been in a fire. What are we going to do?"

"Aaw, man! This is what I've been afraid of. Darren didn't die from the shooting. We didn't realize that until two years later."

"What the hell happened?"

"After the shooting, Darren survived the bullet wounds. We thought he was dead. Once his body was dropped off at the morgue, later on in the night, he waited for the morgue attendant to fall asleep. He was next in line to complete an autopsy. Darren switched his body with someone else's. Ever since then, he's been on the run. I got a court order to exhume his body for DNA evidence for unsolved murders on several islands which was how I found out he was still alive. Needless to say, the DNA didn't match. He's been using Raymond's identity as well."

"That's the name of the guy the receptionist said was at the rehab center."

"Darren has been using the identity of Raymond Gilles. I never told you this, but he was really my brother. Growing up, all of us were so close. When I got locked up, Raymond chose money, greed, and envy over his own flesh and blood. Once he joined forces with Darren, my whole family disowned him. Raymond killed a lot of people for Darren, who had him doing a lot of his dirty work. Darren isn't stupid enough to use his own information to move around. I guess he figured no one would inquire about my brother."

"Why didn't you tell me he was on the loose?" I barked at him.

"I didn't want you or Gabrielle worrying about it. Plus, I thought I could have caught him by now. The country of Trinidad, the DEA, and the FBI have been working together to track Darren down. Every time we think we have him, he moves again. Darren has set up a new team and been moving cocaine in the islands and the Southwest part of the United States."

"Why do you think Darren is posing as Tory?"

"To get back at you and find out who was really behind the shooting of Raymond and him. Ultimately, he wants his power, the real estate properties, and money back. Remember, everything went to Gabrielle and the daughter. His bank accounts were emptied. Darren can't get anything even if he tried."

"The psychologist at Wake Forest in Dallas was murdered."

"It doesn't surprise me. He probably got in the way of him getting close to Tory. Darren killed him to keep his mouth shut. The shrink probably heard or saw something that could have been detrimental to his whole operation. After we located Darren in Texas, the trail got cold. One thing is for sure, those scars aren't from a fire. They're probably from plastic surgery. He probably paid an expensive penny to alter his face and body to look like Tory's. That's probably why you were unable to find him until now."

"Do you think Tory is still alive?"

"First, I need you to take a picture of 'the new Tory' and send it to me through the cell phone. As far as your husband, I'm going to be honest with you. I truly don't know. In the meantime, what I'm going to do is figure out where Darren has set up shop. I've never seen a picture of Tory, so send me a picture of him too."

"All right. Hurry up! Please do whatever you need to do to kill this devil. And, please, spare me the speech. I know I have to act as normal as possible. It will be one of the hardest things I'll ever have to do, but I have no choice but to pull it off."

Tears wouldn't stop pouring down my face. *If Tory is dead, it would be my fault.*

Chapter 59

Despite feeling depressed and defeated by evil, I maintained my role as the good wife. Darren had no idea I was on to him. Five days ago, I'd worked up the courage to give Darren another Percocet for his back pain. Once again, he fell asleep within minutes. Not only did I take pictures of his face, I also took pictures of his entire body, part by part. I uploaded the pictures on the Internet to e-mail to Brennon. I also sent Brennon the most recent pictures of the true Tory Sothers.

While waiting to get word from Brennon on what the plans were, I had a lot of fun fucking with Darren. Knowing he had high blood pressure, I cooked nothing but fatty foods for him. I even fried pickles for him. He couldn't say no. I was hoping to skyrocket his blood pressure and send him into a mini-stroke.

It pissed me off knowing Darren loved being in another man's shoes, another man's life that he didn't deserve. When Darren had sex with me, I bit my lip and closed my eyes tight to stop the tears. I couldn't enjoy the sex with him, now that I knew who he really was. Now, it felt more like habitual rape.

"Where are we going today?" he asked me one sunny Saturday morning.

"We're going to Busch Gardens in Williamsburg. You know how I love roller coasters. Be ready in fifteen minutes."

With him having an irregular heartbeat, he was supposed to stay clear of amusement park rides.

"Nya, I wanted to be home by six o'clock tonight to watch the soccer game."

Tory never liked watching soccer, preferring football, baseball, and basketball.

"We'll be back before your precious game starts. Besides, it's only fifty minutes away from here." I grinned.

"Do you think Michael and Natalie will want to go?" he inquired heading out the house.

I knew he wanted to bring the kids to use them as an excuse to weasel his way out of getting on the roller coaster.

"No, Jarvis and Yvette had a birthday party to take them to."

If I could've helped it, Darren was never going to lay eyes on those innocent children ever again.

Once we got to the park, I immediately wanted to dig into riding most of the roller coasters. We rode the Alpengeist, Apollo's Chariot, Battering Ram, Curse of DarKastle, Escape from Pompeii, Da Vinci's Cradle, Lescoot Flume, and The Loch Ness Monster. A classic roller coaster was The Big Bad Wolf. After riding the Roman Rapids, Darren and I were drenched in water.

After riding the roller coaster, Darren said, "My chest feels tight."

"Aw, baby, you'll be fine! I'm having so much fun," I declared, dragging him by the hand to buy snacks.

The next thing on my list was to fill him up with nothing but sugar, driving him to a dizzy state.

Three weeks later, I was working the night shift in the emergency room. Tonight, the weatherman had forecasted a full moon. For hospital workers, that meant a crazy, chaotic night.

I saw a paramedic rolling a man on a gurney. The man had a bucket of Kentucky Grilled Chicken in his hands.

"What do you have?" I asked.

"Face trauma and a broken nose," the paramedic replied.

The next thing I know, another man showed up in the emergency room with bite marks all over his face, including a bloody ear, and he had a chicken drumstick in his hand.

I asked Donna, "What's with the chicken?"

"Girl, you didn't hear about the free chicken giveaway."

"No, I didn't hear anything."

"Well, KFC, courtesy of a famous celebrity, is giving away their new grilled chicken recipe for free. All you have to do is download your coupon or as many coupons you want from the website. You get two pieces of chicken, a fresh-made biscuit, and two sides of your choice. I stood in line for two hours to get my chicken, using five coupons. I fed my whole family for free." Donna giggled.

"Maybe these two guys got tired of waiting in line."

"I already talked to the police. They were fighting over chicken because one got bigger pieces than the other at the KFC on Providence Road. They started the fight when the place ran out of chicken, and one guy felt the other guy's pieces were bigger. They went to blows about who deserved the bigger pieces of chicken. This is the sixth case I've seen today come through this ER. Not to mention, there have been so many car accidents in the parking lots of Kentucky Fried Chicken restaurants across the country. The parking lots are full, yet they're still cramming to park and get in for free food."

"To be honest, I feel sorry for the workers at KFC."

She nodded. "Girl, I feel for them too."

Suddenly, the two men started fighting again over the bucket of chicken, almost knocking down an elderly patient. I couldn't believe two grown men would cause such a ruckus over some chicken.

I yelled, "Security! Security!"

Chapter 60

"What's the plan?" I eagerly asked Brennon after he sent a text message asking to call him.

Thankfully, Darren was out of town on business. I was supposed to pick him up from the airport later tonight. It'd been one month and eighteen days since realizing I'd been living with the enemy.

"Darren has set his headquarters on the island of Barbados. Right now, he's operating in Texas, Utah, and Nevada. His next move is to Charlotte, North Carolina to reestablish himself on the East Coast."

"No wonder he keeps pitching me the idea for us to move there."

"We think we have located Tory. He's in Barbados. We believe he's been there the entire time, but we don't know for sure yet."

"I can't believe you found him," I announced, jumping up for joy. "I thought he was dead."

"Nya, I need you to focus. Lure Darren to the island, and we'll take it from there. Don't be alarmed, because federal agents will be following your every move. Continue to be patient. This will all be over soon. Despite what's going on, I do have some good news."

"Tory still alive is the best news. How can you top that?"

"Gabrielle is nine weeks pregnant. The doctors said she wouldn't ever be able to have a child. It's a miracle."

"Congratulations!"

"Thanks. I want Darren dead more than you do. I've got a child to protect."

"Thank you for everything, Brennon. Please let me know if you find out anything else. I'll figure out how to get Darren to the island."

I had to do some serious plotting. For now, I still had more ideas up my sleeve to make Darren suffer just a little bit more.

Hector Lavoe, the legendary singer, was honored at a club called Acapulco. I had entered Darren and myself into a salsa dancing contest being held there, knowing he didn't know how to dance. I picked him up from the airport and went straight there.

Needless to say, he kept falling on his ass and couldn't keep up with the steps. We lost the trophy and the five hundred grand prize, but it was worth it to see him sweating profusely and looking stupid on the dance floor. The real prize was seeing him bent over in pain, since dancing was no good for his back problem.

"Why didn't you mention earlier that we were going dancing and that I had to wear that ridiculous costume? You know I've been having back pain, Nya. And you just took me there without even asking me if I was up to it. I've had a tiring day," he said, clearly irritated.

"You've never had back pain before. Why are you having chronic back pain now?"

"I don't know," he shot back quickly.

"Maybe you should go see a doctor and stop giving me an attitude."

"Nya, I'm sorry if I'm giving you an attitude. Perhaps I should go to the doctor and get checked out. For now, I'm going to get out of these clothes and hit the shower. I got another client to sign with the company tomorrow," he announced, heading up the stairs.

Later on we were lying on the couch and watching old episodes of *The Cosby Show*.

I asked him, "How was your flight from North Carolina?"

He nodded. "Productive."

"You've been working so much and really pulling your weight. I'm proud of you."

"Thanks. I appreciate it, especially coming from you."

"You're welcome. I have a surprise for you," I announced, dangling the airline confirmation in his face.

"What is it?"

"I was planning on cashing in my vacation, but after giving it some thought, I decided to use the time instead. I figure we both work hard and deserve a getaway trip. We're going to Barbados. Donna just got back from there with her husband and showed me the pictures. It looks so beautiful."

"Work is hectic—"

"Before you say another word, I've all ready talked to Irv and worked it all out. We leave on Saturday. It's already Wednesday, so you better start packing. We'll be staying at the Sandy Lane Golf and Resort Spa. I've reserved two rounds of golf for you. Barbados, here we come," I said, hugging him.

"I can't wait," he said weakly.

Now that I'd held up my end of the bargain with Brennon, I was hoping that he'd deliver. That night, I dreamt about reuniting with Tory. I felt terrible about him losing a year of his life.

Chapter 61

Saturday couldn't come fast enough. Darren gave me every excuse in the book to cancel the plans to Barbados. Finally, I played the you-owe-me card for everything he put me through as an alcoholic. He didn't have anything else to stand on and eventually gave in.

When we touched down in Barbados, his whole demeanor changed, and he was on edge. From leaving the house to arriving at the hotel, I continued to text Brennon, keeping him informed of our every move. He only sent me back one text from the five that I sent, which went against what we'd discussed earlier. Brennon should have texted me back each time.

After fifteen times, in the hotel room, I was expecting the police, FBI, and DEA to barge in the room and take Darren down once and for all.

Darren paid the bellman and closed the door of our room. "What my Nya wants, she gets." He pulled me close in his arms.

"Darren, how long were you going to keep posing as Tory?"

He froze at first. "What?"

"Did you think I wouldn't notice the many differences between the two of you? For starters, he knows how to please me. You, on the other hand, were off more nights than can I count on both hands." I couldn't resist taking shots at his integrity and pride.

"I befriended Tory in that drug rehab place in Texas. He told me all about you, the alcohol, the precious memories you shared. As you already heard, I'm supposed to be dead."

"It wasn't coincidence that you ran into him."

"Of course not. Once I found out he had become an alcoholic, I knew it would be easier to get rid of him. When he went to rehab in Texas, it gave me the chance I'd been waiting for. I couldn't do it in Virginia. Too many witnesses and prying eyes, especially in your neighborhood. Tory was really into those bars. My good friend Curtis always curled up next to him so they could talk about their problems and drink and drink. One or two in the morning was the usual time he would go back home to you. Eventually, we both learned when Tory was drunk; he would spill his guts about you.

"Slithering my way back into those moist pink walls of yours was the part I enjoyed best. Nya,

Tory doesn't deserve you. He chose alcohol over you, to prove it. After Tory and I were roommates for six months, I realized I didn't need him anymore." Darren had a smirk on his face.

I started to panic. "Darren, you don't get to decide my relationships." *Where is Brennon at? He and the whole cavalry should have been here by now.*

"I know what's best for you."

"Where's Tory?" I screamed.

"Did Brennon tell you he was alive? It pays to have a leak in the FBI. Those daily updates sure come in handy when they're after you. Tory is dead." Darren laughed.

"No!" I yelled, sticking a needle in his chest. He didn't notice when I grabbed it from my back pocket. The double dose of potassium could severely slow down his heart rate. I was able to pass through the airport with the needles and the medicine after I'd informed the airport workers I was diabetic. Under the circumstances, they understood and allowed me to carry the medicine pouch in my purse. I had sent Darren to get me something to drink, to make sure he wasn't around when all this happened.

"What did you inject me with?" he whispered, crumbling to the floor, barely able to speak.

"You have an irregular heartbeat and failed to mention it to me. It's all right though. That's what we have medical records for. I stuck you with potassium. It slows down the heart rate. You're a monster. Hell is too good for you. Oh, I forgot to tell, you, Darren, placing tiny holes in the condom did work. I got pregnant by you. Once I found out, how evil you were, I decided it was best for me to have an abortion."

Just then, somebody kicked open the door. I thought it was Brennon coming to rescue me, but it was Darren's goons. One of them hit me in the face with a bat, and everything went black.

Chapter 62

I opened my eyes and saw Tory, Brennon, and Gabrielle tied to up to some chairs, and surrounded by Darren's two gunmen. It appeared as though we were in an abandoned building. I had a pounding headache. When I tried to move, I realized I was tied up to a chair too.

"Well, well, the whole gang is here," Darren proclaimed as I came to.

"Tory," I called out, tears in my eyes.

"Nya, I thought you were dead," he said.

"I looked everywhere for you."

"I know, baby."

"I love you."

"I love you too."

From my angle, I could see his wedding ring was still on his finger.

"Nya, there was a leak in the operation. Darren found out about it. That's why you didn't hear from me. I told Gabrielle what was going on. I begged her to stay home. But she hopped on the next plane flying out to Barbados," Brennon explained.

Darren caressed her face. "Seeing Gabrielle is an extra bonus."

"Don't touch me!" she hissed.

"Lies and deception will never make a true relationship," I declared.

Darren laughed in a devilish tone. "Both of my women are feisty."

"What the hell do you want from us?" I asked.

"I want my fucking life back. Brennon, if your ass would have just rotted in jail, Gabby and I would still be together. Tory, if you would have never gotten in the way of my happiness with Nya, you wouldn't have been kidnapped. Have you enjoyed your stay for a little over a year with me?"

"Fuck you!" Tory yelled.

"That's what I did to Nya over and over again. Damn! She has some good pussy."

One of the gunmen walked over and quietly whispered into Darren's ear, "Boss, a shipment just came in."

Little did he know, I could read lips.

"Go ahead with the business as usual. There's plenty of money to be made. I got this on my own."

The two gunmen headed out.

Meanwhile, I noticed Brennon desperately trying to free his wrists. Tory and I needed to divert Darren's attention to us.

"Let us go!" I screamed.

Tory mocked me. "Let us go!"

"Nya, do you know how much I lost this past year ducking and dodging the police?"

"No," I replied, shaking my head.

"It's over five million dollars and counting. Years ago, you could have told me my best friend Brennon was hot on my trail, but you didn't. Instead, Nya, you betrayed me. To top things off, today you shot me up with potassium. I almost died in that room." Darren smacked me in the face.

Once Tory saw Brennon unraveling the rope around his wrists, he started doing the same thing, since Darren's attention was all on me.

"If I just had a little more time to stick you in your chest, you would be dead."

"You're lucky I didn't kill you with my bare hands when you told me about getting an abortion. Nya, you know how much I love children. You didn't care and killed our unborn child. To make up for killing my baby, now I will kill your husband. I will give you the choice on how Tory should die. What's it going to be, the knife or one shot to the temple?" he asked, waving a knife in one hand and a gun in the other.

Just then, Brennon quickly rose up from the chair and grabbed the gun from Darren's hand.

Tory, who had managed to free himself too, grabbed the knife and stabbed him in the left eye.

"Shoot him!" I yelled.

Brennon shot him ten times.

Once Tory freed me from the bound rope, I kicked and stomped on Darren's body over and over again, while Brennon called for backup.

"It's over," Tory said.

Within ten minutes, police, DEA, and federal agents were swarming the abandoned house.

All of us were ordered to go to the hospital. Gabrielle and the baby were well, but as a precautionary measure, the doctors wanted to monitor the baby's heart rate for at least one night.

Despite minor bruises on Tory and Brennon, they were discharged. I ended up with a swollen cheek and a mild concussion from getting knocked out with a bat in the hotel room.

"Thank you." Brennon embraced me.

"No. Thank *you*," I replied. Despite the circumstances, it was nice to meet Gabrielle.

The same night, Brennon had the court approve a warrant for Darren's DNA samples. A few days later, Brennon saw Darren's body cremated with his own eyes, wanting to make sure he was dead and that there would be no coming back.

To my surprise, there was a hundred-thousand-dollar reward for the capture of Darren Edmonds. Tory and I were entitled to it. We decided to donate it to all the victims' families.

After cooperating with the police, DEA, and federal agents, it was time to return home.

It turned out that Darren had Tory captive there the whole time, with round-the-clock security and surveillance on his every move. Tory knew of Darren's complete history. He couldn't think of leaving because there was always a gun pointed at his head.

During his year in captivity, Tory had a lot of time to think about his father's death, his family, and me, and took a stand to stop drinking altogether.

We agreed not to tell a soul what truly happened. All we wanted was to move on and look forward to the future.

Epilogue

Tory and I decided to renew our vows and invite our closest friends and family members to the ceremony. No one could tell the difference in Tory, except that his skin had cleared up. Those were the only comments both of us were receiving. The girls wanted to know what magic lotion Tory had used to get rid of his scars.

It was easy for Tory to get back into the groove with his job with Irv and at the restaurant.

Next fall, we will be welcoming a son into the family. His name will be William Martin Sothers. My parents and his mother are counting down the days till I deliver the baby. This whole ordeal has taught Tory and I to appreciate and love each other even more.

Gabrielle delivered a healthy six-pound ten-ounce baby girl named Gina Laura Gilles. Brennon said they couldn't be happier. He and I promised to keep in contact more with each other.

Yvette never came clean about the brief affair she had. With the mother-in-law finally out of the way, she finally has peace in her home again. The relationship between her and her husband is getting stronger every day.

Tara has become a homebody and rarely parties now. Her primary focus is her family. Rob was granted full custody of his son Ryan. With Ryan and Victoria being so young, Tara decided to stay at home with the kids. For Victoria's second birthday, they are planning a trip to Disney World.

My little sister Leah will never change and will forever be a party girl. A couple of weeks ago, I found out her vehicle was on the brink of getting repossessed again. This time, I didn't bother helping her out. She needs to learn to be more responsible and pay her bills on her own.

In the meantime she has Nelson, who continues to put up with her. I can't judge him for staying with her regardless of what trouble she gets herself into. With everything I've been through, I've learned that love can definitely conquer all.